Books by Bill Kincaid
[All are available on Kindle and Amazon]

Ventryvian Legacy

Wizard's Gambit
Kings and Vagabonds

Historical Fiction

Nicodemus' Quest
Saul's Quest
Joseph's Quest
The Making of the President:
The Nightmare Scenario

Humor/Fractured Fairy Tale

Ronald Raygun and the Sweeping Beauty

Drama/Plays

Sweeping Beauty [comedy]
Celestial Court [Christian]

Kings and Vagabonds

A Max Strider Novel

By Bill Kincaid

Kings and Vagabonds is a work of fiction. Names, characters, places and incident are either the product of the author's imagination or are used fictitiously. Any resemblance to actual persons (living or dead), events, or locales is coincidental.

Copyright © 2021 by Bill Kincaid. All rights reserved. Printed in the United States of America. No part of this book may be used or reproduced in any manner whatsoever without express written permission except for brief quotations embodied in critical articles and reviews.

Background

By the end of Earth's twentieth century, telescopes had been developed that were able to find distant solar systems across the Milky Way galaxy, and astronomers had begun cataloguing those new-found entities.

However, actual exploration of other solar systems initially appeared to be beyond the capacity of humans except in science fiction books and motion pictures. The immense distances involved with space travel, when coupled with problems involving the speed and durability of spacecraft, made interstellar voyages virtually impossible.

Though solid and liquid propelled rockets had proven their usefulness in putting satellites into orbit around the Earth and delivering astronauts to the moon, they were not practical for interstellar space travel. Several other concepts were developed—and some were even tested—but all were discarded. Using nuclear reactors to superheat hydrogen was deemed too inefficient, while using small thermonuclear bombs to propel the spacecraft was too risky.

All of them were too slow to be practical. Humans were well into the twenty-first century before they ever built a spacecraft capable of going much faster than 150,000 miles per hour. Until they could exceed that threshold, a spaceship going to Proxima

Centauri, the nearest star to our sun, would take more than 17,000 years to make the 24-trillion-mile journey.

Harnessing nuclear fusion—the energy source of the stars themselves—showed greater promise, though engineers were initially baffled about how they could get rid of all the waste heat that was generated. Midway through the twenty-first century, however, scientists developed ways to rechannel the heat and use it as part of the fuel that propelled the spacecraft, which eliminated the problem of excess heat while increasing the speed generated by the fuel.

What was learned during the experiments with nuclear fusion was merged with developing technology with antimatter and magnetic containment fields. The result was an "annihilation chamber" in which relatively small amounts of matter were converted into almost pure energy.

By the end of the twenty-first century, space probes had been developed that could travel at the approximate speed of light.[1] Hundreds of probes were sent out to the new solar systems that had been found. The probes examined the planets and transmitted data back to Earth at light speed.

Out of the thousands of planets that were probed, sixteen had both water and an atmosphere that was similar to Earth's. Those sixteen planets were listed as being Earth Virtual Equivalents—or EVEs.

---

[1] 299,792,458 meters per second, or approximately 186,220 miles per second

However, water was consistently available in a liquid state on only three of them. One of these was EVE012-MWQ3.28059234, the twelfth EVE planet catalogued—or Eve Twelve, as it was commonly called by those in Earth's Space Exploration Program.

The MWQ3 designation after the hyphen indicated that Eve Twelve was in the Milky Way Galaxy's third quadrant, while 28059234 further narrowed its location on astronomical maps.

Max Strider, an astronaut in Earth's Space Exploration Program, was the only member of his team to survive hiber-sleep during his journey from Earth to Eve Twelve.

Wizard's Gambit told how Max arrived at the planet and got involved in a power struggle for control of Ventryvia, a principal country on Eve Twelve. *Kings and Vagabonds* continues that story.

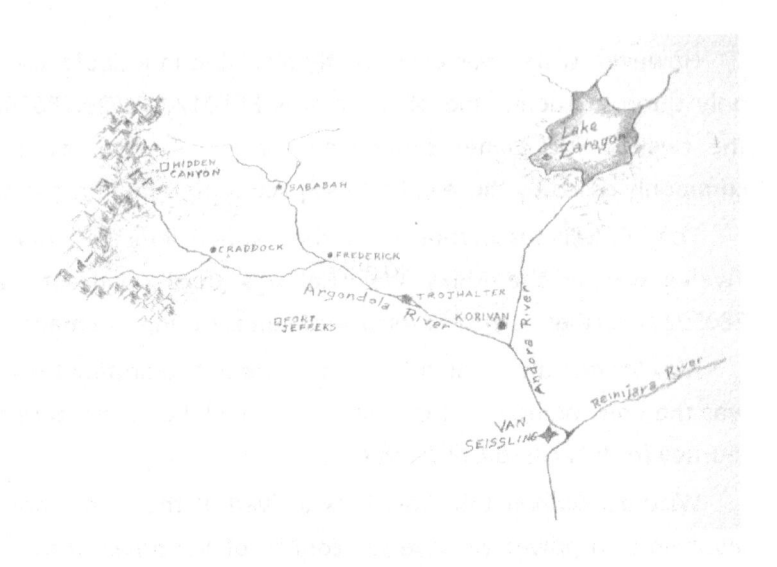

Ventryvian Military Ranks

Ventryvian Rank	Similar to
Premander	General
Requinder	Colonel
Manatar	Major
Royzan	Captain
Sarheit	Sergeant
Reiff	Sheriff

Kings and Vagabonds

A Max Strider Novel

1.

In some respects, it's tedious, almost mind-numbing work—but I've convinced myself it must be done. In a land largely controlled by magic, there is simply too much that can go wrong not to have essential systems backed up by other systems.

Cables therefore connect not only my power generators to the electrical equipment and the solar panels I've installed on the roofs of Ventryvia's palace, but also back up my wireless communication and computer systems.

My private office on the second floor of the palace is the same suite of rooms that had belonged to Wizard Malmortiken, who was second in power before leading his unsuccessful rebellion against King Kylandar. The king had wanted me to be his new wizard, but I'd refused because I don't know how to do real magic.

After considerable pleading by the king, I finally agreed to serve as his engineer. After all, that's what I really am—and is the reason I'm even on this planet. I was sent here from Earth to serve as the engineer on a team of astronauts who were supposed to explore the planet. Unfortunately, none of the other team members survived the journey.

Since I'm virtually indistinguishable from the human-like inhabitants here, they don't know I'm an alien—and I want to keep it that way. The planet's inherent magic allows us to communicate without difficulty most of the time. I don't understand how it works, but I'm glad it does.

I also don't understand how the natives are able to magically do things, but I'm trying to learn. I'm studying scrolls Wizard Malmortiken had in his office that I hope will help me in this endeavor. In the meantime, I've got technology developed on Earth which I do understand—and which is viewed by the natives as my own special form of magic.

I've even had to adjust my thinking regarding inanimate objects. For example, the palace I'm in is a living entity. Although it is formed of hard substances and looks like typical buildings on Earth, it is infused with magic so that it can better look after Ventryvia's king, his family, and support staff. It sees to everyone's comfort and needs (even magically removing their waste products), watching over them in a manner that reminds me of the way a mother looks after her children.

While comparing readouts from the systems I'd installed, I'm interrupted by a knock on my office door.

"Come in," I call.

Young and vivacious Princess Rhylene enters haltingly, a worried expression marring her otherwise beautiful features. She's a few inches shorter than my six-foot frame and would probably be about 25-30 in Earth years. She exudes energy and life in a way like no one else I know. Her lush cinnamon-auburn hair falls to the small of her back, providing a nice contrast to the forest green outfit she wears. Her silver-blue eyes are large and wide as if everything she sees is new and adventurous. They normally sparkle with excitement, but appear a bit clouded today.

"Have you seen or heard from Daddy?" she asks.

"No. Not since he left on his hunting trip. Why do you ask?"

"I was expecting him back by last night at the latest."

I walk to my desk and glance at my appointment book. "I wasn't expecting him back until tomorrow."

"That was his original plan, but he told me as he was leaving that he'd be back two days earlier than officially scheduled."

"Did he say why?"

"No, but I'm afraid something may have happened."

"Have you called him on his transceiver?"

"His what?"

"His transceiver; that thing I gave both of you to wear in your ears."

"No. I forgot all about it."

"Are you wearing yours?"

"N-no," she admits haltingly. Rhylene drops her eyes to the floor before glancing back up, biting her lip and blushing. "I took it out before I went swimming that time

Malmortiken captured me and haven't worn it since. I don't know what happened to it."

"I'll try mine. Vicky, connect me with King Kylandar."

Vicky is what I call the VIC 3700 computer that runs my spacecraft orbiting this planet. It's programmed to vocally interact with humans and was the most advanced computer available when I left Earth on my mission to EVE012-MWQ3.2805, a planet I initially called Eve Twelve—but which I now call home. I don't know yet whether the planet's inhabitants have a name for it. If they do, I don't know what it is.

After a minute or so, the computer notifies me that Kylandar is not answering the call.

"Maybe he's on his way but was simply delayed," I suggest.

"No. I've already used the Farview to check the roads between here and his hunting cabin."

"What's a Farview?" I ask.

Rhylene looks at me with a surprised expression. Then she smiles and says, "It'll probably be easier to show you than to tell you. In any event, it's something you need to know how to use."

She walks to the door, turns back to face me, and urges, "Follow me."

I lock the doors to my office and follow her to King Kylandar's office on the third floor. The Princess walks behind the King's desk and presses a wooden wall panel.

A bookcase slides to the right, revealing a circular staircase inside a tower I had never noticed before.

We climb upward several stories before the stairs open onto a small alcove encircled by windows overlooking the courtyard and palace below. A metal speaker's lectern is on a raised dais in the center of the alcove, and a metal guardrail about waist high is attached to the lectern and curves around the sides of the area where the speaker would stand.

I step up onto the dais and look at the lectern. Engraved into its surface is a detailed map of Ventryvia. Various markings and figures similar to the runes featured in J.R.R. Tolkien's writings cover much of the map, lectern, and guardrail. I straighten my back, standing tall while gazing ahead at the sky and clouds. I have the silly sensation that I am expected to address whatever imaginary audience could be found in the clouds.

"This is the Farview," Rhylene says. "Stand behind me on the dais and watch as I operate it."

I do as she says, standing just to her left, looking over her shoulder at the map.

"Notice that I grasp the bar with both hands," she says as she follows her own instructions. "Since the Farview is directed by one's thoughts, it's not necessary to speak to it—but I will so that you can better tell what I'm doing."

"Take us along the roads leading to Daddy's hunting cabin in the woods," she says.

As I watch in amazement, almost everything around us totally changes. The walls of the alcove disappear, and we appear to be floating through the air on the dais. We're still standing behind the lectern and Rhylene's holding fast to the guardrail, but the rest of the palace has fallen away. The stone walls, the roofs and battlements—all of it have simply disappeared as we fly over the city of Van Seissling.

I gasp and instinctively grab hold of the Princess. She jumps, but then relaxes and grins at me.

"Sorry," I mutter.

"A bit startling the first time, isn't it?" she asks, her eyes sparkling mischievously.

"You can say that again!" I respond, removing my hands from her body and placing them firmly on the guardrail.

We fly above the streets of Van Seissling before moving past the walls and gates of the city. As we approach someone resembling Kylandar, Rhylene moves us in close to him for a better inspection.

"Can he see us?" I ask.

"No. Since we don't physically move from this spot in the palace, none of these people see us—but the Farview's magic allows us to see them."

"Impressive," I marvel.

"The road we are viewing is the highway to Nantanna on the seacoast. It's the route Daddy normally uses when going to or from his hunting cabin."

I relax a bit more, beginning to feel more at ease with what's occurring. After all, I've floated in space high above the Earth—and this feels somewhat like that.

We stay above the highway, about level with the tops of the trees on either side of the road, for what seems like a few minutes—but when I check my watch, I realize it's actually been about half an hour.

Suddenly Rhylene causes the Farview to swoop down closer to the ground. We duck under the canopy of trees and follow a small trail that winds through the forest from the right side of the road. Since the obstructions, thickets, and places along the trail where a body could be hidden are numerous, we examine this area more slowly than when we skimmed along above the highway.

Nevertheless, searching by Farview is much faster than searching on the ground, and we make it all the way to the cabin within the hour.

"I didn't see anybody who even remotely looked like him," a dejected Rhylene says.

"Me neither," I mumble. "Where exactly is this cabin?"

"Look at the map, Max. Do you see the area that's glowing?"

I look and see a spot to the northwest of Nantanna that appears brighter than the rest of the map.

"Is this it?" I ask, pointing to the place.

"That's it."

"Can the Farview check the interior of the cabin?"

"Only to the extent we might see through the windows," Rhylene answers as she angles closer to the structure. We attempt to look through the windows but can see nothing. We then prowl around the exterior and visit the blind Kylandar uses for hunting wild animals.

Rhylene looks up at me and says, "Here. Why don't you take control and get a feel of the Farview?"

We switch places. Putting both my hands on the guardrail, I attempt to mentally direct the magic. It shoots up along one tree before crashing back to the forest floor, but I soon settle down, and so does the Farview.

There's evidence of some animals having been recently tied to the hitching post outside the cabin, and a cart has left ruts through the grass.

"Did your father take a cart or wagon?" I ask.

"No. He rode his sorrak[2], Snowblaze."

"Did anyone go with him?"

"I think Yarrod went along."

"Yarrod? Who's that?"

"He's one of Dad's old friends. They've been talking about getting together ever since Yarrod retired last year."

"Has he returned? Your father might be with him."

"I don't know. I came to see you first, since you were right here in the palace. I'll go to his house here in Van Seissling and find out."

---

[2] Sorraks are similar to horses but have tentacles where a horse's mouth would be.

"I'll go with you."

Rhylene nods, closes her eyes and murmurs, "Back to the palace, please."

The alcove surrounding the Farview materializes as if the mist obscuring it has dissipated. We step down from the dais, descend the staircases, and walk from the palace through the streets of Van Seissling.

When we arrive at Yarrod's house, Rhylene knocks on the front door. After a few moments, an elderly lady opens the door and says, "Why, Princess Rhylene. Please do come in."

"Thank you, but we can't stay. I just want to speak with your husband."

The lady gets a puzzled look on her face and replies, "He's not here. He went hunting with your father."

"When do you expect him to return?"

"I thought he'd already be back, but I haven't seen him yet. Is everything all right?"

"I'm sure it is. Sorry to have troubled you. Whenever he returns, would you please have him contact me? What I need to see him about will only take a few moments."

"All right. You're certain they're doing fine?"

"Sure. Sorry to have bothered you."

We back away and turn toward the palace.

"I didn't mean to upset or worry Margot," Rhylene mutters.

"At least we found out they are both still gone," I respond. "Let me check on something with my computer,"

I say before speaking into the transceiver I keep in my left ear. "Vicky, do you have the coordinates for King Kylandar's hunting cabin?"

"Yes. I got them while you were viewing the cabin with the Farview," the computer responds.

"As soon as I pick up some items from the palace, I'll need you to transport me there so I can look around."

"Not by yourself!" Rhylene interjects. "I need to come, too."

"Better not, Princess. It could be dangerous."

Rhylene grabs my arm and glares at me. "He's my father, I'm coming along, and that's final."

I hesitate, and she grips harder.

"All right," I reluctantly agree.

A few minutes later I instruct Vicky, "Transport us to a spot near the cabin—but be ready to pull us back out if we run into something we can't handle."

2.

We materialize in a small clearing surrounded by massive trees. It takes me a moment to orient myself and find the trail leading through the woods to King Kylandar's cabin.

I check the settings on the blaster I hold in my right hand, nod to Princess Rhylene, and we move stealthily down the forest path. Approaching the place where we can see the cabin from the trail, I tell Rhylene to stay hidden as well as she can while moving forward toward the clearing surrounding the structure. I warn her to remain in the trees until I signal her or call her on the new transceiver I've given her.

While reconnoitering the area with the Farview, I had noticed that the cabin's north wall contained a large fireplace and no windows. I therefore work my way stealthily through the trees toward that side and approach from that direction. I cautiously creep to a window and peek in. Everything is dark inside and there's no one in sight.

I quietly make my way to the door and check the handle. Unlocked. I push it open, step in, and look around, using the beam from my tactical flashlight to assist me. I see nothing unusual in the front room or in the corner containing the kitchen stove and sink.

The bedrooms are a different story. The beds in both rooms are rumpled and unmade, bedcovers asunder and lying across the floor. I see no one in the cabin.

I walk back out onto the front porch, retrieve my fingerprinting kit from my backpack, and dust the handles and knobs on the door. After transferring the prints I find into my portable data computer, I signal Rhylene and she comes running.

"Put these on," I say, handing her a pair of disposable kylarex gloves. "Don't worry. I'm wearing some, too." I show her my gloved hands. As she puts hers on, I add, "Tell me if you see anything out of place or different from the way your dad normally keeps the cabin."

She looks at me quizzically, but nods that she understands. I push open the door, and we step inside. When I snap on my flashlight, Rhylene jumps and spins around, surprised.

I flash a mischievous grin at her. "A bit startling the first time, isn't it?"

"You can do it your way, but I prefer this," she answers, holding out her hands as a luminous ball of light floats upward from them, illuminating the room.

"Show off!" I exclaim.

She just smiles but studies the room. "I think Daddy may have been interrupted or may have had to leave suddenly."

"What makes you think that?"

"Well, just look at this room. His bow and quiver of arrows are over there in that corner. Coats are thrown across the couch, and there are dirty dishes all over the tables. Daddy always insists that we straighten up the cabin before leaving."

Rhylene glances around one more time before walking from the living room into the larger of the two bedrooms. Shaking her head, she exclaims, "Daddy would never leave his room in this condition if he had time to straighten it. I'm positive something unexpected happened."

I look at the room. King Kylandar's transceiver is lying on the nightstand next to his bed. That explains why he didn't answer my call, and it means I can't use it to track his location. Next to it is a glass containing a small amount of liquid. I pull out the glass rod I use to determine the chemical components of liquids, stick one end into the glass, and say, "Vicky, I need you to analyze this."

"Will do," the computer responds through my transceiver.

A few minutes later Vicky reports, "The liquid is wine with strong traces of morphine and another chemical I can't identify."

We look around the cabin and find another glass with a little dried liquid residue in the bottom, but it fails to register on my rod. I seal the glass in a kylarex bag before putting it into my backpack. Next to the kitchen sink is an almost empty bottle of Pinot Gran Mountjoy.

"That's probably Daddy's," Rhylene says. "It's his favorite wine."

As I start to collect fingerprints from the bottle, Rhylene asks, "Please excuse my asking, but what are you doing?"

"I'm collecting fingerprints."

"You're doing what?"

"I'm making a copy of the fingerprints on this bottle."

"I don't understand."

"Temporarily take off one of your gloves and look at your hand. Do you see the tiny ridges on your fingertips?"

She nods.

"When you grasp hold of an object, some of the natural oils in your hands are transferred. By lightly dusting it, I can see a copy of your fingerprint."

"What good is that?"

"Your fingerprints are different from mine—and from your dad's—and from the person or persons who abducted him. If I can identify that person's—"

"Abducted?" she gasped. "Do you really think someone abducted him?"

"Sorry. You're right. We don't really know that."

"But that's what you think, isn't it?"

"Well, uh—"

"Be honest. I'm an adult."

"Yes, Rhylene. That's what I'm assuming. He's not here in the cabin, and we checked the hunting blind and other places around the cabin with the Farview."

She hesitates, nods, and says, "I fear you're right. But why would someone do it?"

"He's the king. It could be an attempted coup, or ransom, or to get information, or all sorts of reasons."

"So how does getting fingerprints help you?"

"If I can identify that person's fingerprints, I may be able to prove he or she was involved."

"How do you know what other peoples' fingerprints look like?"

"Well, I don't. At least, not yet."

"So you don't have copies of anyone else's fingerprints?"

"No, not yet."

"Then I don't see how it will help."

"It may not, but this may be the only chance we have to get this evidence—and could come in handy if we can get the other person's prints later."

She shrugs and sighs, "If you say so."

After collecting prints from the bottle, I pour part of the contents into another glass and have Vicky analyze it. The chemical composition is identical to that of the liquid in Kylandar's glass.

We carefully examine the cabin, looking for clues, but I see nothing that helps me. Kylandar's and Yarrod's clothes are scattered around the rooms, supporting the theory they were abducted, but useless for helping us find them. We scoop up loose objects we find—such as buttons, coins, slips of paper, pieces of cloth, and other miscellaneous items—and seal them inside small kylarex bags.

After making one final pass through the cabin, we turn our attention to the exterior. Some type of animal—probably the sorraks belonging to Kylandar and Yarrod—have recently been tied to the hitching post in front of the cabin, and it's evident that other animals pulled a cart or wagon up near the front porch. It also appears that the animals hitched to the post were then tied to the cart and led away.

I photograph and measure indentations in the grass, and we follow them toward the main road.

"What's that?" Rhylene asks, pointing at something fluttering on a thorn bush between some trees. We walk toward it and discover a ripped piece of cloth. The grass and weeds appear to be slightly trampled.

"It looks as if something has been dragged through the underbrush," I remark.

"Or someone," Rhylene suggests.

I nod and we move forward, following the crushed grass, weeds and underbrush.

As we press through some bushes, we see a man lying in a pool of blood.

"Oh no," gasps Rhylene. "It's Yarrod."

I kneel beside him and check for a pulse, but find none. His throat has been cut, and his heart appears to have stopped after losing a massive amount of blood. Since his body is rather stiff, I assume rigor mortis has set in. I find myself wishing our chemist, Dr. Cynthia McNamara, had not died while our spaceship was travelling to this planet.

"Whoever killed him did it right here," I say to Rhylene.

"How can you tell?"

I point to dried blood coating the leaves of bushes near him. "When he was first cut open, his blood was able to shoot that far."

I take pictures and gather as much evidence as I can from the scene of the crime. We search the immediate area but find no sign of Kylandar. We also find no evidence of any other trampling of underbrush or similar signs indicating another body had been carried elsewhere. I therefore assume Kylandar is in the cart or wagon, though we have no way of knowing whether he is dead or alive. I take heart, however, that we spotted no more blood.

We return to the trail and follow the wagon tracks until they intersect the main road. Two wagon wheels left ruts in mud that has since dried, and I make a digital polymer impression of the ruts, save the readout to my portable data computer, and upload it to Vicky.

Rhylene bends down and closely examines one of the sorrak prints. "This one was left by Snowblaze," she says.

"How can you tell?"

"His shoes are marked with the royal seal."

I switch my focus from the red highlights in her auburn hair to the hoofprint in the mud. I drop to my knees to look at the impression. The iron shoes fitted to sorraks' hooves are similar to horseshoes back on Earth except that they have a wider point at the apex of the shoe. Instead of being a plain area, each of Snowblaze's shoes have a crest bearing the royal seal.

"By golly, you're right!" I exclaim and make another digital polymer impression of Snowblaze's hoofmark, saving it as before.

From the marks left by the cart as it cut across the corner before merging with the road, I can see they headed south toward Nantanna.

"Do you think Daddy's still alive?" Rhylene asks with a quiver in her voice.

"Almost certainly," I respond with more optimism than I actually feel. "We know he was alive at the cabin, but he's no longer there or anywhere around it. Since his body's not here with Yarrod, we can assume his captors abducted him for some other purpose—probably for ransom or to extract information."

"We've got to free him before they do something dreadful to him. Let's use the Farview to see if we can find them," Rhylene suggests.

"Good idea. Although there may be plenty of carts and wagons on this road, I'll bet there won't be any others that have Snowblaze attached to it."

I speak into my transceiver, "Vicky, transport us to the palace. Also, send any available probes to Nantanna and the area around it. See if you can find Kylandar, Snowblaze, or the cart that's transporting them."

3.

"You're much better at using the Farview than I am," I tell Rhylene as we arrive at the palace. "See what you can find on it. Use your transceiver to contact me if you discover anything."

"Where are you going?"

"I'm going to check video images my computer may have caught that could help us. If I have time, I'll also do an analysis of the samples we collected."

"If you have time?"

"Yeah. I hope you find them on the Farview before I get that far."

Rhylene looks at me with a question in her eyes—but instead of asking it, she nods, turns, and races up the stairs.

I adjust the backpack containing the samples we collected, go to an isolated room where I'm hidden from other people, and ask Vicky to beam me up.

"We need to determine the approximate time of Yarrod's death," I tell Vicky when I arrive at my spacecraft. "Do you have any programs that can do that? You know, from rigor mortis or something?"

"I am programmed for necrochemistry."

"What's that?" I ask.

"Post-mortem chemistry. It's a biochemical analysis of the dead person's tissue, blood, urine, and cerebrospinal fluid. I can transport Yarrod up here, and you can collect the samples for me to analyze."

"Sounds good, but I have no idea about what samples are needed or how to get them."

"I'll print out instructions while bringing him up."

"Thanks, Vicky. Do it."

"Yes, sir."

We beam Yarrod's body up, and I move it to the ship's clinic. I also discover something I didn't know about my own sensibilities. Collecting samples of Yarrod's blood and urine cause me no problems, but I'm somewhat squeamish about puncturing his eyeballs to draw out the vitreous humor.

Somewhat squeamish? All right, let's face it. I'm totally freaked out by having to do it. But since the vitreous resists putrefaction longer than other body fluids, I force myself to do it anyway.

When Vicky finishes analyzing the various fluids, the computer reports, "Yarrod died between seven and eight hours ago."

"Thank you, Vicky. Let me see a map of where our probes are located,"

Two probes are positioned above the highway leading to Nantanna, and four others are within the city itself.

"Pull up the video for the last nine hours recorded by probe VF1825," I order. I have only watched for a few minutes when I spot a wagon being pulled by a team of sorraks, with two sorraks tied to the back of the wagon. I run the video back and watch the individual relevant images. I choose five pictures, enhance them, and print and save them.

I do the same thing for the more southern probe on the road to Nantanna. I make three more prints of the wagon and save both the prints and the full sequence of video images showing the sorraks and wagon.

An examination of the video showing the city gates of Nantanna fails to show the wagon and sorraks. A second watching verifies their absence.

I study my map of the city. Nantanna's only gates are the main gate and the rear gate that opens onto the wharves, but that area is blocked off from the land surrounding the city by walls.

After pondering the significance of the missing wagon, I print a map of southern Ventryvia and mark the positions of the two probes when they recorded their pictures of the wagon. Then I scoop up the map and prints, walk to the transporter room, and tell Vicky to beam me back to the palace.

4.

As I get to the top of the stairs leading to the Farview alcove and look through the doorway, I am greeted by an incredible sight. Rhylene is standing on the dais operating the Farview, but that's all I can see. She, the lectern, the railing and the dais are all floating in midair. Everything else on the other side of the doorway is gone.

I grab hold of the doorway's facing, lean as far as I can through the opening, and look around. The castle in which I am standing and to which I cling appears to have vanished.

"This is crazy!" I mutter. *No,* I mentally correct myself. *It's not crazy—It's magic. Earth rules don't necessarily apply here, so get over it. And get on with what you need to be doing.*

"Rhylene!" I yell to her.

She turns, looks toward me, and apparently gives some kind of mental command that causes the castle's walls and the floor of the alcove to reappear. She acknowledges my presence with a smile.

"Find anything?" I ask.

"Nothing of any importance. But then again, I'm not sure I know what I'm looking for—other than Daddy and Snowblaze, of course."

I walk forward and hand her the pictures of the wagon and sorraks. "See if this helps."

She examines the pictures closely and murmurs, "Yes, that's definitely Snowblaze. But where's Daddy?"

"Probably in the wagon. Do you recognize the man driving it?"

"I don't think so. Of course, it's hard to tell when only looking at the top of his head. Do you have any from any other angle?"

"Unfortunately, no. We're lucky to even have these."

"You're right," she admits. "It's definitely more than what I've found so far. I've been looking all over Nantanna but can't find anything."

"I don't think they went to Nantanna."

"You don't?"

"No. I think they turned off before reaching the city gates. I've checked the pictures of the traffic going through Nantanna's main gates, and none of them show this wagon and sorraks."

"Where and how did you get these pictures?"

"I have probes over key areas of Ventryvia. These pictures were taken by two of them over the main highway to Nantanna. Since they show the wagon and Snowblaze but the pictures from Nantanna's gate do not, it's likely they turned off south of here," and I point to a red dot on the map I prepared of southern Ventryvia.

"I presume these two red dots mark the probes' locations?" she asks.

"That's right."

The princess examines the map, turns, and walks back to the Farview, taking the map and pictures with her. I follow.

Rhylene guides the Farview to a point slightly north of where the last sighting of the wagon and sorraks was made before moving us along the road until the vegetation and other markings line up with those in the pictures from the probe.

"See if we can find where they turned off," she says.

"Roger."

"Who?"

"Never mind. It's just a slang expression meaning I agree."

She gives me a quizzical look, shrugs, and turns back to the Farview. We stay over the central portion of the road watching for intersections.

The first such intersection is with a road branching off to our left.

Rhylene stops the Farview and asks me, "Which way?"

"Go along the new road to the east but look for recent wagon ruts."

After about two minutes, we come to a lower area which is still slightly muddy. We zoom in closer and study it in detail.

"People have walked through here recently and have ridden sorraks," I comment, "but I don't see any wagon tracks."

"Neither do I. Nor do I see one of Snowblaze's prints."

"Let's go back to the Nantanna highway."

Rhylene nods and complies.

After a few more minutes, we find another road heading east. We follow and discover it leads to a small village. We examine all wagons and sorraks in town, but none match those in my pictures. Although there are several sheds offering cover from the weather, we are able to examine them sufficiently to determine neither Snowblaze nor the wagon are there. The only building in town that could conceal them is a blacksmith's shop. The road does not continue beyond the village. We return to the Nantanna highway.

The next intersection is with a road leading west. We follow it for several minutes before finding a muddy low spot that holds marks of people passing. The problem is that it contains too much information. It's too heavily travelled. Although remnants of wagon ruts and sorrak hoofmarks are abundant, they are so numerous that we are unable to match any to the impressions I made.

We continue along the road until it forks.

"Which way?" Rhylene asks.

"Take the right fork, since it appears less travelled. Maybe any markings we find will be less likely to be obscured by more recent traffic."

After a few minutes, we come to a low spot covered by water. Wagon wheels, sorraks, and boots have left their marks in the mud on both sides of the water. One set of wagon wheels looks similar to the ones we are looking for, but none of the hoofmarks match Snowblaze's.

"What do you think?" I ask.

"I don't know. I want to believe this might be a match, but I don't want to waste precious time."

"I agree. Why don't we check the left fork? If we don't find a match there, we can come back to this spot. We could even have Vicky transport us here in person for more precise measurements."

"Sounds good," she agrees, and moves us back to the fork in the road.

We follow the southwestern road until it comes to a small town. We search the town but can't find either Snowblaze or the wagon in my pictures. We do, however, find seven stables and a blacksmith shop where they could be hidden.

We continue on and five minutes later we come to a patch of mud at the right side of the road. Zooming in, we see the clear markings of a sorrak's hoofmark that contains the royal crest.

"Snowblaze!" Rhylene exclaims.

"Vicky!" I almost shout into my transponder. "Are you following our progress?"

"Yes, sir."

"Send any flying probes you can spare along this road. See if you can overtake the wagon and men who abducted Kylandar. Send some of the probes farther down the road to whatever town or village it leads to."

"Yes, sir."

I turn back to the princess. "Continue searching with the Farview while I call N'Shawn."

A startled expression races across her face before being replaced with an understanding nod.

"Contact N'Shawn," I say into my transceiver.

The sounds of static are quickly replaced by a voice. "This is N'Shawn."

"Max Strider here. Where are you right now?"

"I'm on the outer wall of Van Seissling."

"What about the King's Regiment?"

"It's guarding the two inner walls of the city. Two other regiments guard the outside wall, with a third regiment held in reserve."

"Put your men on alert. I also need to visit with you later about a possible problem."

"What kind of problem?"

"You'll find out when we meet."

"When and where?"

"I'll contact you but be prepared to meet me later today in my office."

"Yes, sir."

I terminate the conversation and turn back to Rhylene. "You'll need to be at the meeting, too."

She nods that she understands.

"Have you found anything else?" I ask.

"No. I've just been continuing down this road but haven't found any other tracks."

We search for about an hour before finding additional hoofmarks left by Snowblaze. The wagon and sorraks had apparently encountered a rainstorm, which is both good and bad for us. It's good in that the marks we find confirm that Snowblaze passed this way. But other markings and impressions have been washed away by heavy rain that fell just a little way down the road.

We continue to search for several hours but find nothing. Vicky confirms that the probes we've sent out have not encountered either the wagon or Snowblaze.

I tell Vicky, "Move as many probes as you can spare into this area. Keep constant surveillance on this part of Ventryvia and notify me immediately if you find anything."

"Yes, sir."

I turn to Rhylene. "Are you ready to meet with N'Shawn?"

She sighs wearily and says, "I hate to give up on this—but we've probably done about all we can do with the Farview. At least for now. It might be time to call in reinforcements."

"Yeah," I agree. "Plus some other things. Let's go to my office before I call N'Shawn."

5.

I look across my desk at Rhylene. I want to pick her brain on a few matters before calling N'Shawn to join us. "What do you think happened to your father?"

"It appears rather obvious to me that he was abducted."

"Why? What's the motive or purpose?"

"As you pointed out to me when I asked you that question, he is the king. Maybe someone wants to seize the throne."

"Internally like a military coup? Or externally like an invasion?"

She hesitates before answering, "I—I don't know. Have you seen any evidence of either of those happening?"

"Not yet," I answer. "But that's why I want to explore the possibilities before having N'Shawn join us."

"You don't think he's behind the abduction, do you?"

"Not particularly, but a great deal of power is concentrated in a country's armed forces. Consequentially, it's wise for a ruler to keep an eye on his military. How loyal are our troops—and their commanders?"

"I'm not sure about all our soldiers. It hasn't been that long since many of them were fighting against Daddy as part of Wizard Malmortiken's rebellion. But I trust N'Shawn, and Daddy does, too."

"Your father also trusted Malmortiken and considered him his closest friend."

"That's true, but the wizard coveted power. I don't think N'Shawn does. At least not in the same way."

"Is one way better than another?"

"Well, N'Shawn wants sufficient power to win a battle, but he doesn't covet power for the sake of having power—or to rule the country."

"Is there any reason we shouldn't tell N'Shawn everything we know?"

She pauses before answering, "I'm hesitant to let it be generally known that Daddy is missing and very likely abducted, but N'Shawn is commander of our troops. I think he must know. What do you think?"

"I agree. If he's loyal to your father, he needs to be kept in the loop—especially if someone's trying to seize the throne."

"*If?* What other motive could there be?"

I ponder the question before answering, "Ransom, revenge, destabilizing the country. All sorts of things are possible, including the fact that several armed Resistance groups were fighting against Kylandar only a year ago."

"But the Resistance joined with Daddy to fight against Wizard Malmortiken."

"Only Barlowf's group. There might be others that still think your father was responsible for the problems caused by Malmortiken. They may still be in rebellion."

Rhylene opens her mouth to say something, stops, and silently nods.

I continue, "But almost all of the things I've mentioned are areas where N'Shawn's expertise could help—provided he's loyal to your father and you."

She nods, smiles, and says, "Call him."

When N'Shawn arrives, he takes a seat next to Rhylene in front of my desk. We fill him in on what has happened, telling him both what we know and what we suspect, and give him copies of the pictures of the wagon.

"So you want me to put my troops on alert, but don't want me to tell them why," N'Shawn summarizes.

"That's right," I respond. "We don't want confusion or panic, especially since there may be some logical reason for the king's disappearance. But we need to be prepared in case someone is plotting an invasion or coup."

"You think someone could be plotting either one?"

"We think it's possible."

"Any invasion threats?"

"No. Not that we're aware of, anyway."

"Any troop movements?"

"No."

N'Shawn sits thinking for a moment before saying, "I agree, but I think it might be wise to expand our network of intelligence gatherers and spies."

"Do you already have such a network?"

"I'm head of the military. We always have at least an informal one. For example, we've been watching some of the Resistance groups that were fighting against King Kylandar while the wizard was running things."

"Are they still in rebellion against him?"

"Not openly, but a couple of them haven't disbanded. So we're still keeping them under surveillance."

"Visit with your agents. See if any of them have seen or heard anything, but don't tell them the king is missing. As for expanding the network, think through what you have in mind, and get back with us. For that matter, come up with any other suggestions you think may help, but be sure to keep Princess Rhylene and me in the loop. We need to give final approval until Kylandar returns. Do you agree, Rhylene?"

"Yes," she replies.

"I understand and will do anything I can to get your father back safely, N'Shawn says. "Is there anything else?"

I glance at Rhylene, and she shakes her head. "Not at this time," I say while standing to shake his hand.

6.

Rhylene and I continue searching for her father for the next three days, the princess on the Farview while I use both it and video feeds from various probes. Despite our best efforts, we find nothing of consequence.

Then on the fourth day, I get a message from Vicky.

"Sir, I think one of our probes may have found something."

"Send it to my office screen."

The center screen on my back wall comes on and displays an image of four men riding sorraks on a road. One sorrak is a white charger that looks like Snowblaze, and his rider appears to be King Kylandar. Two of the men with him are armed with bows, quivers of arrows, knives and lances.

"Where is this?" I ask.

"They have just turned onto the highway between Nantanna and Van Seissling."

"Turned on from where?"

"A probe caught them riding through one of the villages on the road you and Princess Rhylene have been searching together on the Farview."

"Can you show me on a map?"

"Yes sir," Vicky responds while turning on the left screen on my office wall.

I print two copies and rush upstairs to the Farview. As expected, Rhylene is using it to search for her father. I give her one of the maps and ask her to move the Farview to the spot shown on the map.

She zooms in, carefully studying the rider on the white sorrak.

"That certainly looks like Daddy," she says. "But where's he been, and who are those men with him?"

"For that matter, why are they with him?" I ask.

"I don't know." She pulls the Farview in close to each man in turn. "Wait a moment! This one looks like Haughton!"

"Who?"

"Haughton. Daddy's butler."

"You mean the guy who drugged him under Malmortiken's orders?"

"That's the one."

"That makes no sense. Why would he be with someone who betrayed him?"

"I don't know. We may just have to wait and see what they have to say—if they even come here. These men might just have an amazing resemblance to Daddy and Houghton."

"See if the white sorrak's hoofprint has Snowblaze's royal crest," I suggest.

"Good idea."

Rhylene moves the Farview close to the ground where the white sorrak is walking. After several minutes we see a good impression of the sorrak's hoofmark, bearing the royal crest.

"Snowblaze!" she says.

"But who are the other two men?" I ask.

"I don't know. I've never seen them before."

"Whoever they are, they're heavily armed."

"Maybe Daddy's a captive, and they're guarding him."

"Maybe—but if that's the case, why would they risk moving him openly down a public road in the daylight?"

"You're right. That doesn't make sense, does it?"

We're both quiet for several minutes before Rhylene breaks the silence. "We could provide our own escort for Daddy."

"Who do you have in mind?"

"The Dragon Company."

I nod approvingly, "Well, they're the best fighters in our army and are fiercely loyal to your father—but let me check something first. Vicky, check our probes across Ventryvia to see if you find any invasion forces or similar military groups that could be setting up a trap for our military if we expose them."

"Yes sir" the computer responds.

A few minutes later Vicky reports, "Nothing out of the ordinary, sir. Of course, we don't have probes in all locations, and enemy soldiers or insurgents could be disguised."

"Understood. Contact N'Shawn."

The initial static is replaced by, "This is N'Shawn."

"A man who looks like King Kylandar is riding Snowblaze up the Nantanna Highway toward Van Seissling. He is accompanied by three men, one of whom appears to be Haughton, who betrayed the king to Malmortiken last year. They should reach Van Seissling sometime this afternoon."

"Is there anything you want me to do?"

"Be prepared to have the Dragon Company intercept them. I'll keep you informed of any developments."

"Yes, sir," N'Shawn says as he signs off.

"You decided not to intercept them now?" Rhylene asks.

"Yeah. This whole situation strikes me as being odd. It may be more prudent for us to use the Farview to watch them without their being aware of our presence."

Rhylene frowns, thinks for a moment, and says, "You may be right."

We watch as they turn onto the trail leading to Kylandar's hunting cabin, follow it a short distance, and stop near the location where Yarrod was killed. One of the heavily armed men leaves the others on their sorraks while he goes to the spot where Yarrod had been slain. When he can't find the body, he yells to the others and they help him search the area. They find blood on the leaves and underbrush, but no body.

After what appears to be a frantic discussion, the four men ride to the cabin, tie their sorraks to the hitching post, and go inside. They return after a few minutes, again have a short discussion, and get back onto the sorraks. They ride back to the main road and head north toward Van Seissling.

Rhylene turns to me and asks, "What was that all about?"

"I'm not sure other than it seems obvious they were expecting to find Yarrod's body."

"But why?"

"They know he was killed. Maybe they were planning to bring his body back home with them."

"Maybe," she agrees without sounding convinced.

I notify N'Shawn when they get within fifteen minutes of Van Seissling, and he rides out with the Dragon Company to meet them.

7.

Rhylene and I continue to watch as the Dragon Company advances on and surrounds the king's party of riders. Although N'Shawn salutes Kylandar as his soldiers approach, the two men guarding the king appear to react hostilely, with one of them starting to draw his bow while the other acts as if he might flee. Kylandar says something to them, however, and they settle down, though they still seem nervous.

As the group passes through the outer gates of Van Seissling, Rhylene and I return from the Farview's alcove. The princess is almost giddy with excitement as we descend the stairs. We reach the second floor just as Kylandar and his men enter the palace.

"Daddy!" Rhylene shouts as he passes through the front door, abandoning all pretense of reserve as she rushes to meet him.

Although he initially looks shocked, he quickly recovers and scoops up his daughter in his arms, twirling her around with a big smile while exclaiming, "Hello, Princess."

"Oh, I was so worried about you, Daddy!"

"Whatever for? You knew I went hunting."

"Yes, but you were due back days ago."

"True, but things don't always go as planned. Hey! Look who came back with me! You remember my old butler, Haughton, don't you?"

Haughton holds out his arms as if expecting a hug when Rhylene stiffens and asks, "Where'd *he* come from?"

Haughton freezes and looks uncomfortably at the king.

"Come now, Rhylene! That's no way to treat an old friend like Haughton."

"Friend? That was before he put drugs in our drinks."

Haughton exchanges a nervous glance with Kylandar before dropping to one knee. "I'm sorry, princess. Malmortiken assured me that you would not be harmed provided I did what he commanded. I now realize that what I did was wrong and ask you to please forgive me."

Rhylene just stands there, listening and thinking but not relenting.

The king stands up straight, rubs his hands together, and says, "Well, I decided life is too short to continue to hold grudges—especially against old friends who have been with me for years. Let's go on up to my office. I've been away longer than planned and need to get back to work."

As he walks past me at the head of the stairs, I bow slightly and tell him, "Welcome back, Your Majesty."

"Uh, thank you," he says before walking on up the next flight of stairs. He is accompanied by Rhylene,

Haughton, and the two guards. I watch them until they pass from view, and then turn and go to my office.

8.

"It's so good to have Daddy back home safely," Rhylene gushes when she stops by my office later in the afternoon.

"It's also good to see you more relaxed and less worried," I respond.

"Well, of course I am! Searching for Daddy and worrying about his safety has pretty well consumed all our time and energy since he disappeared."

"Did he say where he'd been?"

"No. He didn't bring it up. I started to ask a couple of times but decided against it."

"Any particular reason?"

"Not really. I just had a feeling that he didn't feel like talking about it. At least not while everyone else was present."

"Did the others stay in there with him all the time you were there?"

"Yeah. And they're still in there. Daddy and I didn't have any time just to ourselves. Maybe we will later."

"Maybe."

"And I don't know what the eating arrangements will be now that we have a butler again."

"What were they previously?"

"Haughton would normally serve Daddy and me in one of the dining rooms. If we had dignitaries, we often ate in the formal dining room. If it was just the two of us, we might meet in a less formal alcove or in the kitchen, sometimes in the library. Of course, since you've taken Malmortiken's place, you've generally eaten with us."

"Did Malmortiken join you back before his open rebellion?"

"Sometimes, but he didn't place a high priority on it except for a few months after Mom died."

"That was while he was consolidating his power, wasn't it?"

"Yeah. Afraid so."

"Please keep me posted on anything you find out or learn, but don't do anything to make it appear that you're trying to learn information."

"Why? What is it you want me to find out?"

"Nothing in particular. Just be on the lookout for information we should know."

"Come on, Max. You're fishing for something. Why are you suspicious? And of what?"

I sigh, shake my head, and sigh again before answering. "Your dad comes back with two guys we've never seen before. Plus a man who betrayed him. Not to mention a good friend of his has been murdered, and no explanation for any of this has been given. Well, not except for the importance of not holding grudges against friends. I want to watch, listen, learn, and hopefully find out to what extent—if any—we can trust these men who have accompanied the king back to the palace."

"And you also want me to watch, listen, and learn?"

"Yes, provided you can do it without endangering yourself."

"I'll try," Rhylene says as she smiles and leaves the room.

I sit down at my desk and think. *King Kylandar has his personal secretary, Fitzroy—or at least he did before those three new guys came back with him. Rhylene has her personal handmaid, Lady Lillian. Both Fitzroy and Lillian act as door keepers and run interference for their bosses. Who do I have? No one except my computer. Granted, Vicky's a tremendous asset. But I could probably use someone to assist me as a personal secretary.*

What about security? If those two new goons come barging in here, do I have anything that could stop them or even slow them down without causing too big a scene? Not really. The best I could do is hope Vicky could get me out quickly enough.

What if they come nosing around while I'm not here? If Kylandar is in their power, there's no telling what they could or would do.

I could spend virtually all my time elsewhere—like on my spaceship or at Hidden Canyon. But that might leave both Rhylene and Kylandar at their mercy. If they even have any mercy! No, it appears I've got a bunch of things that must be done around here, and most of it is way more important than the cables I was connecting before Kylandar went missing.

9.

"Hello," Rhylene says to me as she stops by my suite of rooms after supper. "Mind if I come in?"

"Please do."

After relocking my door, I lead the way across the room and we sit down around my desk. "What's happened since I last saw you?"

"Haughton informed me that dinner was ready. I went downstairs to the dining room, and was met by Daddy, Bynum, and Carzikon. Those are the two guys who came back with Daddy."

I have her repeat the names while I write them down. "Will you be eating with them again tomorrow?" I ask.

"Probably."

I get up, walk to my closet, get several kylarex bags, and hand them to Rhylene. "If you can get something like a cup, glass or silverware handled by Bynum or Carzikon, please do so provided you can do it without being noticed by anyone else."

"That finger whatchamacallit thingy?"

"Yes. I want to check fingerprints."

"I'll try."

"Thanks. Please go on with what you were saying before I interrupted you."

"Daddy had soldiers bring up beds to his outer chamber for Bynum and Carzikon."

"They're going to be sleeping in his office?" I ask.

"No, the office is the first room in. Well, actually the first three rooms in. There's a front office, Daddy's personal office, and a small third room often used for storage, which is where they'll sleep. Next comes the outer chamber, and then there's the inner chamber where Daddy sleeps."

"Why's he putting them there?"

"He claims he's hired them to be his personal bodyguards."

"Personal bodyguards—but you've never seen either of them before?"

"Not that I recall."

"Sounds like they're going to continue watching him closely. And probably watch us as well."

"Probably."

"Does Kylandar seem comfortable with this arrangement?"

"As nearly as I can tell. Daddy just says he was gone longer than he meant to be and is busy trying to get caught back up again."

"Has anybody mentioned Yarrod yet?"

"Not yet. I probably would have if you hadn't cautioned me not to do anything that could endanger us."

"Understood. Does Lady Lillian stay with you all the time?"

"No. She did until she married Jamistan, but now she's only here while working during the daytime."

"Then be sure you keep your door locked and bolted. And don't open it unless you know who is there."

"Is that really necessary?"

"Yes. We don't know whether we can trust those guys who came back with your father."

"Very well, but you need to heed your own advice."

"I am, Princess," and I point to a video screen on the wall that shows the hallway outside my door.

"Impressive! Could you put one in for me?"

"Probably. I think I have an extra screen and mini-cameras at my place in Hidden Canyon. It may be a few days before I can get them—provided you're sure you want them."

"I'm sure. Please do it. And thank you."

*****

"May I come in?" Rhylene asks, knocking on my door the next day.

"Of course," I answer as I unlock the door and let her in. "What's up?"

She reaches into her purse and pulls out two kylarex bags.

"This knife and fork are Bynum's, and the goblet and other knife are Carzikon's. I used a napkin to pick them up. Hope that helps."

"Thank you," I say while putting on a pair of gloves and retrieving my fingerprinting kit. I dust the items brought back by Rhylene and examine the prints. Some are smudged or indistinct, but others appear to be of good quality.

"I'll see if these match any of the prints we got from the cabin. If you're able to get more, please continue to collect them—provided you can do so safely."

"I'll try," she says, heading for the door.

10.

"The few fingerprints on the silverware that are distinct enough to use for identification do not match any from the cabin," Vicky tells me. "But some of the prints on the goblet match some from the wine bottle."

"Aha! So Carzikon was at the cabin!"

"Maybe, but those might be King Kylandar's fingerprints. We know he was there."

"Oh, drat! You're right. We need to get his— Wait a minute. Did we get copies of Kylandar's prints last year while we were checking to see if he was being drugged?"

"No. We only did chemical analysis of his food and drink."

"You still have the results, don't you?"

"Yes, sir, and I'm printing a copy now."

As I look over the printout, Vicky adds, "As you can see, morphine and another chemical compound I can't identify were placed in his wine."

"Why can't you identify the second chemical?"

"Since it's not something we have on our database, I don't have a name for it. However, the chemical composition and diagram of the molecular structure is on the printout."

"Thanks, Vicky. Can you also do a printout of the chemicals that were added to the king's wine bottle at his cabin?"

"Certainly."

About a minute later, Vicky prints a second paper.

"Holy cow!" I exclaim. "The chemicals are the same as what was added to his wine last year."

"Yes, sir," Vicky confirms. "Even the relative strength of the chemicals is the same."

11.

"When we watched the video of Haughton adding drugs to your father's wine last year, we saw him put in measured amounts of the individual drugs to your father's goblet," I tell Rhylene while installing miniature cameras outside her door.

"So?"

"So I think it's significant that the strength and proportion is again the same this time—even though this time it was added to a bottle of wine instead of to a goblet."

Rhylene's puzzled expression is quickly replaced with understanding.

"Ah—because it means the person who did it this time is using the same recipe."

"Exactly! It's very likely the same person this time around."

"Haughton?"

"Haughton!"

"Which may be the real reason he came back with Daddy."

"But why is your father putting up with it?"

"I don't know. Here at the palace he is surrounded by his own forces—people who are fiercely loyal to him."

"Maybe he's being drugged again."

"Maybe. But if he is, I don't think it's the same way or the same drugs."

"Why's that?"

"Well, Daddy seems mentally sharp this time, rather than being muddled or lost like before."

"Perhaps he's being controlled some other way. I guess it's even possible that we're letting our imagination run wild, and there's really nothing sinister going on—"

"No!" Rhylene interrupts. "I'd be tempted to believe that if only Yarrod hadn't been murdered. But seeing his throat slashed like that and his blood . . ."

She squeezes her eyes shut, shakes her head, and shivers.

"No. There's something else going on. Are you willing to continue helping me try to figure it out, Max?"

"Of course."

"Your suggesting that it might just be our imagination made me wonder."

"No, Rhylene. I am also suspicious and don't really think we're imagining things. Part of the reason I said what I did is that I wanted to see what you'd say. But I also hate to rain on your parade when you were so upbeat and happy yesterday."

"I *was* happy. Happy to have Daddy back. But he's surrounded by people I don't know and can't trust. One of his long-time friends has been murdered, and he seems unconcerned about it. I would think he doesn't know about it except that *we saw him* stop at the place Yarrod was killed. I—I just don't know what to think."

"Are you going to continue to eat with your father and the others?"

"Probably. It's my best chance to observe him and be with him."

"True, but it also places you at risk."

"Don't worry. I'll just continue being Daddy's simple know-nothing daughter."

"Good luck. I hope you can pull it off. If you wear your transceiver at all times and give Vicky permission to monitor you and assist you if needed, we may be able to protect you."

"Thank you. That would help. I'd also like a glass rod if you don't mind."

"You mean the rod for analyzing the chemical composition of your food and drink?"

"Yes."

I go to my office, get an analyzing rod, and bring it back to Rhylene. I finish installing the video screen, connect it to the cameras, and show Rhylene and Lillian how to operate the equipment.

"Now you can keep your door locked and bolted but see who is outside." I reach down and pick up the painting I'd taken off the wall before installing the video screen. "Don't forget to hang this picture on this nail so that it hides the screen before opening the door to someone else. Call me if you need me."

12.

I spend the next couple of hours in my office looking through Wizard Malmortiken's scrolls of magic but am unable to find any information on the chemical compound that was put into Kylandar's wine besides the morphine. My search is interrupted by a knock at my door. The video screen shows the person to be N'Shawn. I unlock the door and invite him in.

"Come on in and have a seat."

"Thanks, but I really can't stay but just a moment. I just wanted to stop by before leaving town."

"Where are you going?"

"King Kylandar just ordered me to take the King's Regiment and the Dragon Company to Trojhalter until further notice."

"What's happening at Trojhalter?"

"We're to keep an eye on Lord Larciby."

"What about the rest of the troops?"

"I'm no longer in charge of them."

"Who is?"

"Premander K'Shay."

"K'Shay? Wasn't he part of the rebellion against King Kylandar?"

"Yes, sir. He was the number two man in the army but served Wizard Malmortiken. However, he *is* an outstanding soldier and leader. He should do a great job."

"But a year ago he was in rebellion against Kylandar!"

"True, but only because he feared the wizard's power. Malmortiken had threatened K'Shay's family. Anyway, King Kylandar just gave me the word. Before I left the palace, I wanted to tell you so that you'd know where the Dragon Company and I had gone. In case you want to reach us. Also, I wanted to thank you for letting me get to know you and to work with you."

"The pleasure is mine, N'Shawn."

He reaches up to his left ear, removes his transceiver, and tries to hand it to me. I refuse to take it.

"If you don't mind, I'd prefer for you to keep it. We may need to get back in touch. Unless, of course, that causes you to disobey a direct order."

"Neither King Kylandar nor Premander K'Shay mentioned it." We share knowing glances and smiles before N'Shawn adds, "And neither did I."

"Did Kylandar say why he reinstated K'Shay and promoted him to premander?"

"All he said is that he's trying to reunite the country, heal wounds that had been caused by the rebellion, and put good people back where they belong—provided that they swear absolute allegiance to him."

"What about your rank? Are you still premander?"

"Yes. Both K'Shay and I are the same rank, but I now serve under his command."

He stands and we shake hands. "Well, gotta go. I'll see you around, Max."

"I certainly hope so," I reply.

13.

"Why would your father send his best and most loyal troops away from here?" I ask Rhylene after telling her what N'Shawn told me.

"I don't know," she responds. "Perhaps something is happening in Trojhalter we don't know about. But it seems especially curious he'd do it at the same time he places the armed forces under Wizard Malmortiken's second in command."

"And the wizard's highest-ranking commander to survive the rebellion."

"True."

"That makes at least two traitors who have been reinstated to key positions. Why?"

"Daddy's explanation both times is that he wants to reunite the country, put the wizard's rebellion behind us, and put good people back into positions where they can effectively use their talents."

"Does that sound like your father?"

Rhylene thinks for a few moments before answering.

"Well, Daddy is good at bringing people together. That may be the key reason he was the right man for defeating the powerful warlords who controlled Ventryvia for so many years. He was able to work with the leaders of various factions, even though some of them couldn't stand some of the others. Daddy looks for common interests and builds on them to form viable alliances. He looks for ways to put people's talents to good use. So I'm not particularly surprised that he brought K'Shay back into service. But I am surprised that he put him above N'Shawn."

"Why's that?"

"N'Shawn is both a good, close friend and is probably more loyal to Daddy than any other man in the army. He's also a great leader of the troops, is quite intelligent, and is good with strategy."

"How does he compare with K'Shay?"

"Well, K'Shay is also a good leader and commander, but I'd much rather have N'Shawn watching my back and protecting me."

"Do you think—"

I'm interrupted by a knock on Rhylene's door. The video screen I've installed shows Yarrod's wife standing outside in the hallway.

As Rhylene gets up, she looks questioningly at me and whispers, "It's Margot. What should we do?"

"Let her in—but be careful not to tell her what we know."

The princess goes to the door, unlocks it, and invites her in.

"Please have a seat, Margot."

"Thank you. Sorry to bother you, Princess Rhylene, but I stopped by your father's office to get some information and wasn't satisfied with the answers I got."

"Please tell us about it," Rhylene urges.

"As you know, Yarrod left with the king to go hunting. Your father returned, but my husband hasn't. I wanted to find out why, so I naturally came here to ask him."

"Naturally."

"Well, at first he wouldn't even see me. Fitzroy announced my presence to some sullen man I'd never seen before who was in Kylandar's office. He passed it on to your father, who said he was too busy to see me today. Fitzroy asked the stranger to urge the king to see me as a favor to an old friend. Kylandar agreed but said it would be a little bit before he could.

"When I finally got in, he simply said Yarrod had left the cabin and hadn't returned. He said he'd waited and waited and had looked for him—but didn't find him. He said he doesn't know where he is or what has happened to him. I asked if he has his military or police forces looking. He looked pained and embarrassed, fumbled a bit for words, and finally admitted that he didn't, but promised that he would. He then thanked me for coming, walked me to the door, and told me goodbye. And that was that.

"Yarrod and I have been close personal friends with Kylandar for decades. He's almost been like a son to us. I really think we're entitled to better treatment and consideration than that. Don't you?"

She sits back, pats her lap, and looks expectantly at Rhylene.

"Yes," the princess agrees while glancing at me. "You definitely have a point."

"Is there anything you can do?" Margot asks.

"I don't know, but we can try."

"Thank you," Margot says. Her eyes plead as she adds, "I'd appreciate it so very much if you would."

Standing up and backing toward the door, she again thanks us and apologizes for bothering us. She reminds me of a little lost kitten.

Rhylene closes the door gently and leans her head against it while taking several deep breaths. She lets out a big sigh and locks the door before turning back and facing me. She looks as if she's been run over by a truck.

"Well?" she asks.

"You look devastated."

"I feel devastated. I hate not being honest with Margot after she's been like a grandmother to me. What do you think we should do about Yarrod?"

"I don't know," I confess. "I hate to tell her he's dead, and we don't have a clue who killed him."

"Especially since we're not sure who to tell."

"Or even to let anyone know how much we know."

"How much *do* we know?" Rhylene asks.

"We know your father and Yarrod went hunting together, Yarrod was brutally murdered, and Kylandar disappeared for a while before returning in the company of a man who betrayed him a year ago."

"And two other guys I don't trust any further than I could throw this palace," Rhylene adds.

"We also know Kylandar and probably Yarrod were drugged before the abduction and murder."

"Using the same formula of drugs as Haughton used last year."

"And he's back now," I say.

"True. Is Daddy being drugged again? He appears mentally sharp, but somehow things just don't seem to be adding up."

"Is there a way you could visit with him privately?"

"Without his new constant companions? I don't know. What would be the purpose?"

"To give him a chance to tell us if he's under some threat or is being controlled or coerced in some manner," I say.

"If I can do it, should I tell him what we know?"

"I don't know. I'd normally tell your father almost anything, but there's something about this entire situation that makes me hesitant. What do you think?"

"I feel the same way. It's great to have Daddy back, but his words and actions make me suspect he might be under someone's control somehow. So how should I handle it?"

"Maybe you can say you want to talk to him somewhere in private. If he agrees, just visit without completely spilling the beans."

"Spilling beans?" The princess looks at me as if I've lost my mind.

"Sorry. Just a slang expression that means telling everything you know."

"So you want me to talk with him in private but not let him know what we found while looking for him?"

"That's right. Wear your transceiver and let me listen in to your conversation and record it."

"Record?"

"Yes. Kinda like the videos I made earlier, except this would just be your voices instead of including visual images. Would that be all right with you?"

"That's probably a good idea in this situation."

I go to my office, get a portable miniature microphone, turn it on, and help Rhylene hide it in her hair.

14.

From the comfort of my office, I listen as Rhylene walks down the hall from her suite of rooms to her father's offices on the third floor of the palace.

"Hello, Fitzroy," she says. "I'd like to see Daddy."

"Just a moment, please," Fitzroy responds as he scoots back his chair and walks to the office door. He knocks, waits a moment, and then says, "Princess Rhylene would like to speak with her father."

An unfamiliar voice tells him she'll need to wait a bit. A few minutes later that same voice announces that the king will see her now and leads her through the outer office and into a second office.

"Hello, Princess," King Kylandar says.

"Hi, Daddy."

"What do you want to see me about?"

"I just want to talk with you a few minutes *in private.*"

"Carzikon," says Kylandar, "would you please leave us alone?"

I hear a door closing.

"Now, Rhylene, what do you want to talk about?"

"I'd like to talk somewhere I know we're totally alone, like in the royal gardens."

"You want to walk down three flights of stairs so we can talk in the royal gardens rather than here in my private office?"

"Yes, Daddy. I do. And it's only two flights of stairs."

Kylandar lets out an exasperated sigh, and then another one before I hear the scraping of his chair as he moves back from his desk while muttering "Smarty." A door opens and the king says, "Come with us, Carzikon. We're going downstairs to the royal gardens." As they pass Fitzroy's desk, I hear Kylandar say, "We'll be back shortly."

"Very good, sire," Fitzroy replies.

I hear footsteps for the next several minutes, but nothing is said as they walk down the stairs and out the rear doors of the palace to the royal gardens.

"Stand here at the entrance, Carzikon," Kylandar says, "and don't let anyone intrude on our privacy."

"Yes, sire."

"Now, what's this all about?" the king asks a few minutes later.

"I just wanted to ask if you are all right."

"You made us walk all this way just to ask *that?*"

"It's important, Daddy. I need to find out if you're being held prisoner."

"Prisoner? Honey, I'm right here in my own rooms in my own palace! How could you possibly think *that*?"

"You're constantly being watched by these two guys none of us have seen before. The only other man who is in frequent contact with you is someone who betrayed you and drugged you only a few months ago. I think I have a right to be concerned."

"I—" Kylandar starts before pausing and thinking for a moment before continuing. "I guess you do have a reason to think that, honey. Let's sit down on this bench over here and talk."

"Thanks, Daddy."

"Is there any other reason that causes you to think I might be someone's prisoner?"

"Well, you were gone several days longer than we thought you'd be, we didn't know where you were, and Yarrod didn't return with you."

"Anything else?"

"You seem more nervous than normal. Of course, part of that could be because you've surrounded yourself with traitors."

"Traitors?" Kylandar questions before lapsing into silence. "All—all right, Rhylene," the king eventually stammers. "I didn't want to tell you this because I don't want to concern you, but I am being forced to do a few things."

"So you *are* a prisoner."

"No, not really a prisoner—at least not in the normal sense. But I am being coerced to do some things against my will."

"Who's doing this, Daddy?"

"I don't know, Rhylene. I don't know who's behind this, but I'm afraid not to do as they direct me."

"You're the king, Daddy. In your own palace and surrounded by your own military and police. How can someone be forcing you to do something against your will?"

"They've made it clear to me that my friends and family are in mortal danger if I don't do as they say."

"Who, Daddy?"

"Mostly you, Rhylene. You're the only family I have left. I can't take a chance on losing you. Especially since they haven't really demanded that much, at least not yet. So I've been playing along with them, doing what they've required until I can find out precisely who they are and where their leader is located."

"You mean *I'm* the reason you are their prisoner?"

"I wouldn't exactly put it *that* way . . . Well, I guess maybe you are."

"Oh, golly, Daddy! Maybe it would be better if I were no longer around."

"No, Rhylene. I'd hate to do that to you . . . Although—"

The king is silent for a couple of moments before continuing, "Is there some place you could go where you'd be completely safe, and nobody could find you?"

"I don't know, Daddy, but there might be. I'd have to think about it."

"If there is such a place and you were able to get there secretly, I might be able to break from their control."

"Let me think about it, Daddy."

"You do that, Rhylene. Do that."

15.

"At least we now know that Daddy is being coerced to do some things he'd rather not do," Rhylene says when she comes to my office.

"Yes, that's what he says."

"You don't sound convinced."

"Sorry. I'm just having a hard time imagining who can frighten King Kylandar that way."

"Would you feel differently if one of your long-time friends had been murdered while vacationing with you?"

"I don't know. Maybe, but I'd probably be mad enough to resist them instead of bowing under to them once I was back in my own palace and surrounded by guards and military."

"What if they were threatening the only family you have remaining? Would you consider playing along until you can find out who and where their leader is?"

"Yeah, that might make a difference. Especially if what I was being forced to do didn't particularly go against my principles."

"Do you think we should disappear for a while?"

"Where do you have in mind?"

"Maybe that place you took Daddy and me to last year."

"Hidden Canyon? Yeah, that might work. Is that what you want to do?"

"I think so. At least for a while."

"All right. Let's go to your room and gather your things."

"What about your things?"

"That's my home. I keep more items there than here."

Rhylene fills several bags with clothes and personal items, and Vicky transports us to Hidden Canyon, a hideaway I'd constructed in western Ventryvia when I first arrived on this planet. I help her carry her things as we walk around the lake and pass behind the waterfall at one end. I put my right hand into a recess in the rocks, and a scanner reads my fingerprints.

A panel of rock slides aside, we walk into the hallway, and lights automatically come on, lighting our way.

"Welcome," I say to the princess.

"Thanks. This place never ceases to amaze me."

We carry her things into the same bedroom she and Lady Lillian used last year, and then I go to my office to get to work. I place my right hand on a scanner, say

"January suborbital configuration," and the computer screens mounted on one wall come on.

I tell Vicky, "Let me see visuals from all probes on the third floor of the palace."

"We have two stealth probes plus the mini-cameras outside Princess Rhylene's door," Vicky says as the images being transmitted by them appear on screen. "We also have eighteen other probes in and around other parts of the palace."

"Thank you. Get some stealth probes into King Kylandar's chambers. At least one in each room."

"Yes, sir," Vicky replies.

"Monitor and record the bodyguards and keep me posted of anything I need to know. I especially want to know who is controlling King Kylandar, how they're doing it, and who is behind this entire operation."

"Yes, sir."

A couple of hours later Vicky informs me that we now have stealth probes in the first two rooms of the king's suite of offices.

"I was able to move the ones on the third floor into place while King Kylandar and Carzikon were eating their evening meal. Stealth probes are so small and move so slowly it'll take another day or two before I can get all the ones in you asked for."

"I understand. But move the one in the office into the bodyguards' bedroom. I want to hear what they say to each other, since they may tell us what we want to know.

You said Carzikon ate with the king. What about the other goon?" I ask.

"Goon?"

"The other bodyguard Kylandar hired to protect him."

"Bynum?"

"That sounds right."

"He's not in any of the rooms. I haven't seen him the past two days."

"Do a search for him, Vicky. His absence might not mean anything—but then again, it might. Was there any discussion about Rhylene and me being gone?"

"There was about the princess. Haughton pounded on her door several times to tell her dinner was ready. He then reported to the king that Rhylene did not come to the door. King Kylandar responded that she may have gone somewhere and ordered that her food be served to her when she returns."

"I heard my name," Rhylene says from the doorway. "What's happening?"

I repeat for her what Vicky told me, show her the video feeds, and explain what I'm trying to find out. Then we head to the kitchen to get something to eat for supper.

16.

The next afternoon Rhylene and I are checking video feeds when Bynum arrives back at the palace. His shoes are dusty, his hair is windblown, and he's carrying a small suitcase, which he takes into the king's office. I assume he gives it to Kylandar, since he comes back out a few minutes later without it. He walks over to Carzikon, who is sitting at the desk in the front office. The two men converse for several minutes, but they do it so quietly that I'm unable to hear what they're saying. Bynum unsheathes and checks the sharpness of two knives. He's apparently dissatisfied with one of them, because he takes it into his bedroom and comes back with a different one.

As he walks down the stairs, I ask Vicky, "Do we have any flying probes that can watch him?"

"Yes, sir," Vicky replies. "I'm sending you a video feed on screen three of the probe I'm assigning to him."

The right-hand screen comes on just as Bynum and Haughton walk out the front door of the palace. The princess and I watch from above as they walk through the inner gate of Van Seissling and through various streets of the city. Haughton seems to be leading the bodyguard.

"Where are they going?" I ask.

"They're heading into an older residential part of town, but I don't know where— Wait a minute! I think I recognize this place. Oh, dear!"

"What is it?"

"This is Yarrod's and Margot's house!"

Bynum hides on one side as Haughton knocks on the door. Margot comes to the door, sees Haughton, talks to him momentarily, and then appears to invite him in. As the butler sweeps past her, Bynum steps forward from his hiding place, pushes Margot fully into her house, and closes the door.

A few minutes later Haughton comes through the front door by himself and starts walking back the way they'd come.

"Who do you want the probe to follow?" Vicky asks.

I look at Rhylene and she shrugs that she doesn't know.

"Stay with Bynum," I reply. "Keep the flying probe on him any time he's outside the palace until I tell you differently."

"Will do."

Nothing happens for almost twenty minutes. Then Haughton returns with some clothes. A few minutes later the two men come through Margot's front door. Bynum is wearing the clothes Haughton brought him, and he's carrying the clothes he had been wearing.

"Zoom in, Vicky," I say. "I want a closer look at those clothes."

They have large blood stains on them.

"I think I'm going to be sick," Rhylene says.

"I may be, too—if they did what I think they did."

"Poor Margot. Why would they do that to a poor old defenseless lady?"

"Silencing her is more important to them than her life."

"Do we know she's dead?"

"I can check."

Rhylene shudders, sighs, and says, "I'm going with you."

"You just admitted this is about to make you sick."

"It very well may. But Margot's a friend. If there's any way I can save her life . . ." The statement is left hanging, unfinished.

I grab my backpack, we walk outside to the meadow, and Vicky transports us to Margot's house.

"Whoa! Hold it!" I yell while grabbing Rhylene as she rushes for the front door. She gives me a look that's part questioning but mostly annoyed. "Don't touch anything until we both put on gloves."

Rhylene sighs but obediently puts on the kylarex gloves before knocking on the front door. No answer. She grabs the door knob, twists, and it yields to her touch.

"Margot?" she calls through the opening. Again, no answer.

She pushes the door open, steps inside, and I follow.

It takes a moment for my eyes to adjust to the gloom of the dark front room, but the smell immediately warns me that our suspicions are correct. The sticky, almost metallic odor assails my nose as soon as the door is opened, and my stomach threatens to do gymnastics on the spot. Margot's body lies crumpled on the floor, surrounded by a pool of blood. The princess gasps, lets out a soft cry, and starts to reach for her friend.

"Don't touch her!" I cry. "I want to record the evidence first."

"She's my friend, Max. I've got to see if there's anything I can do."

"You can see she's not breathing. The best thing we can do for her is to bring her murderers to justice. Step back for just a couple of minutes."

"Minutes?"

"I mean moments."

I quickly take pictures of the room and of Margot from various positions. Then I step forward and feel for a pulse. As expected, there is none. I make digital polymer impressions of the wound where a knife sliced her throat and of a footprint left in blood on the floor next to her.

We look around the house to see if we can find any other evidence. In the kitchen we find a bloody knife that had fallen between the sink and a cabinet. I put the knife into a kylarex bag and go back and get samples of Margot's blood and of the blood on the floor.

After searching through the house but finding no other evidence pertaining to Margot's murder, I have Vicky transport us back to Hidden Canyon.

"We've got to warn Daddy about how dangerous his bodyguards are," Rhylene says. "Now that I'm no longer staying in the palace, he needs to have them arrested before they kill him or someone else."

"Will he believe you?"

"He will if I can show him our evidence."

"Do you think that's wise?"

"Max, he's my father. I'd never forgive myself if those awful men butcher him—especially if I could have prevented it by warning him."

"I understand. It's just that I'm wondering if it might not be better to find out who's controlling him and how. You know, *before* we tip our hand about what we know."

"By the time we find out the answers to those questions, it could be too late."

"All right, second question: How can you present the evidence so that he'll believe you?"

"What convinced both of us before—as well as the Resistance fighters—was watching your video images. If you'll let me borrow it and show me how to use it, I'd like to show him the images on that picture machine of yours."

"The computer monitor?"

"Whatever you call it."

"Let me analyze the knife we just collected first."

"What do you want to know?

"I want to check fingerprints and blood samples."

"In your office down the hall?"

"No. In a lab I have at another location."

"I want to come with you."

"Not this time, Rhylene. The lab is set up so that only I can enter it, but I'll be right back."

She scowls but lets go of her momentary anger, nods, and says, "Hurry back."

When I return, I tell her what I've learned.

"Margot's blood is on the knife, which means it's the murder weapon. The fingerprints are different from those on the bottle but are the same as some prints on Bynum's knife and fork, which you collected earlier. It appears to be the same type of knife as the one that killed Yarrod, though I can't narrow it down any further than that."

"In other words, we know that Bynum murdered Margot and may have also killed her husband," Rhylene summarizes. "And Haughton helped him."

She looks expectantly at me, and I nod.

"I've got to warn Daddy."

17.

Rhylene again wears both her transceiver and a hidden microphone when she seeks an audience with her father. She might not need them, since I have a couple of stealth probes in his suite of rooms and am moving others closer to that part of the palace. However, there are still places I don't have any probes yet, such as in either Kylandar's offices or his bedroom. Microphones and transceivers also give the huge advantage of providing Vicky with precise coordinates in case the princess needs to be transported out of there with little or no advance notice.

I again listen as she tells Fitzroy she wants to see her father, and he announces her to Carzikon. Once again, she is required to wait outside for several minutes.

"Hello, princess," Kylandar says when she is finally admitted to his office.

"Hi, Daddy. I need to talk to you in private."

Kylandar groans, shakes his head, and pleads, "We are in private. Are you going to make us walk all the way down to the gardens again?"

"No. I think it will be sufficient if we go into your bedroom."

"At least that's less inconvenient than the other, though it's still unnecessary."

"Humor your easily frightened daughter."

"Anything to avoid all those stairs."

I hear the scraping of chairs and the closing of a door.

"What is it you want to discuss, Rhylene?"

"I just want to make sure you know how dangerous the men who came back with you are."

"Dangerous? What do you mean?"

"They just killed Margot."

"Who?"

"Margot. Yarrod's wife; the lady who was like a second mother to you."

"What . . . what are you talking about?"

"Bynum and Haughton just went to Margot's house and murdered her."

"Nah. They couldn't have."

"I'll show you."

"Show me? How?"

"Here. See for yourself."

A moment of relative silence followed by, "Where and how'd you get these pictures?"

"Shhh. Just watch, Daddy."

"I'm watching, but all I see is Haughton and Bynum standing outside some house. Oh, all right, outside Margot's house—before going inside and shutting the door. That doesn't prove anything . . . Now they're coming out carrying some clothes . . . Make that carrying some bloody clothes. But what caused . . . ? Oh—oh, dear. Margot? Is that you?"

I hear Kylandar's strained breathing for a minute or two.

"Where and how did you get these pictures?"

"You know how, Daddy."

"I do?"

"Of course. Max did it."

"Max?"

"Same as last year when Max helped you defeat Wizard Malmortiken."

"Ooooh, yes. That way. Of course. Uh, may I keep these pictures? So I can confront them?"

I'm sorry, Daddy, but I must return this device to Max. And be extra careful when you do confront these evil men. Be surrounded by soldiers you fully trust when you do it."

"That's a good idea, princess. I'll be sure to do that. And thank you for the warning."

"You're welcome, Daddy. I don't want anything to happen to you, 'cause I love you."

"I love you too, Rhylene."

I hear a door open and close, and then a second one. As Rhylene comes out of Kylandar's office, she is picked up by my probe and I watch her progress as she makes her way through the remainder of the king's chambers and out into the hallway.

She walks to her room on the third floor of the palace, passes through the door, and relocks it. When she says, "Ready," Vicky transports her back to Hidden Canyon.

18.

"At least Daddy has now been warned," Rhylene says when she gets back.

"Yes, but we are no closer to discovering who abducted your father or who has been controlling him. And if he arrests Haughton and the bodyguards, we might never know."

Rhylene is silent for a minute or so. Then her face screws up a bit and she mutters, "Whoa."

"What is it?"

"I only saw Carzikon and Daddy. I didn't see Bynum."

"Probably in their bedroom. Vicky, is Bynum in the bodyguards' bedroom?"

"No, sir," Vicky replies in my transceiver. "Right now he's riding a sorrak toward Nantanna."

An image of Bynum appears on the center screen at my office.

"How— Why do you have these images?" I stammer.

"You told me to keep that flying probe on Bynum whenever he's outside the palace," Vicky replies. "So I have."

"Bless you, Vicky!"

I turn to Rhylene and say, "It's possible he could be going to meet up with his bosses. If so, Bynum could lead us to the ones who are controlling your father."

"Can we remotely watch the place he goes?" Rhylene asks.

"Good idea. Vicky, bring in additional flying probes and position them around the place Bynum goes."

"Will do. And sir, you should probably look at this."

Vicky sends a video feed to my left monitor. Carzikon has just used a key to open the door to my office on the second floor of the palace. Holding the key in his left hand and a sword in his right, Carzikon cautiously advances through first the office and then my other rooms.

"Is he looking for you, Max?" Rhylene asks.

"I suspect he is. But why is he in my private rooms?"

"I don't know, but it doesn't appear to be a friendly visit."

"Definitely not" I say as he ransacks the drawers in my bedroom. "Why is he fascinated with *that*?" I ask as he closely examines my underwear.

"Probably because he's never seen anything like it before. What is it?"

"Just underwear." And it suddenly dawns on me that my underwear is undoubtedly different from what is worn on this planet. I'd matched my outer clothes but had failed to do that with the garments that are not normally seen. I glance at the princess.

She looks at me suspiciously and says, "Where'd you get that, anyway?"

"I think it's more comfortable than the stuff most guys around here wear. Rats! He just took one of my transceivers!"

Carzikon leaves my rooms carrying a transceiver, an undershirt, and a pair of briefs.

"Vicky. Totally disable the transceiver he's carrying."

"Yes, sir. It's disabled."

"Keep the feed on him running live."

We watch Carzikon walk down the hall, go up the stairs, and enter the king's offices. He passes through the outer office and enters Kylandar's private office. A man I haven't seen before is sitting behind the king's desk. He's a foot shorter than Kylandar, has black hair, a rather large nose, and dark olive brown skin with numerous scars.

"Max isn't in any of his rooms, but I found these things," Carzikon says, and passes the items over to the other man. He examines all three items closely and says, "Thanks. Now go back to your post."

Carzikon exits Kylandar's office and goes back to his own desk in the outer office.

"Have you ever seen that man before?" I ask Rhylene.

"Not that I recall. What's he doing in Daddy's office?"

"I wish I knew."

19.

"That same man's in your father's office," I say to Rhylene the next day. "Are you ready to do what we discussed?"

"I'm ready if your probe's in place."

"It's now in the front room of your quarters, and it shows that the coast is clear."

"What coast?"

"I mean, uh—no one's in your room."

"Then I'm ready to go."

"You'll need to go out to the meadow."

"Why there?"

"Because that's our designated transport point."

She sighs, makes her way to the meadow, and then is transported to Van Seissling. I watch on my computer screen as the princess materializes in her room at the palace. She checks herself and then uses her transceiver to contact me.

"Do you have full visual and vocal contact?"

"All systems seem to be operating correctly," I answer.

"Then let's see what happens."

Rhylene leaves her room, walks down the hall to Fitzroy's desk, and tells him she wants to visit with her father. Fitzroy gets up, walks to the door of King Kylandar's outer office, and knocks.

"Princess Rhylene would like to talk to her father," Fitzroy tells Carzikon when he opens the door.

"Just a moment."

I watch the video images provided by my stealth probes as Carzikon relays the message to the strange man sitting behind Kylandar's desk.

"All right," he responds in a high tenor voice. "Tell her it will be a little while."

Carzikon closes the door, walks back to the other door, and tells Fitzroy. Meanwhile, the strange man opens a drawer in the king's desk, takes out a hip flask, and takes a deep drink of the liquid inside. Almost immediately a transformation begins taking place. He grows taller and his hair changes from black to brown. His skin becomes lighter and smoother while scars disappear, and his nose shrinks and ceases to be mangled. In short, within minutes he grows into the very image of my friend, King Kylandar. If I hadn't witnessed the change with my own eyes, I would swear he *is* the king. The transformation slows down and then stops. The man sits still for a moment, and then rises and walks to a closet door and opens it. He closely looks at himself in a full-length mirror attached to the back side of the door, nods, turns and grabs trousers off a hanger in the closet. He changes into the longer pants before closing the closet.

Walking to the door to the outer office, he opens it and tells Carzikon to admit Princess Rhylene. Then he sits back down in Kylandar's chair behind the king's desk.

"Hello, Rhylene," he says as she walks into the room.

I note that his voice has deepened and changed its inflections so that he now sounds just like King Kylandar.

"Oh, Daddy! It's so good to see you," she says as she runs to him and hugs him tightly.

"Really?" he asks with a bemused grin. "It hasn't been all that long."

"It seems like it to me. Maybe because I've been worried about your safety."

"I'm perfectly safe here in my office, which is in my palace in the heart of my capitol."

"No, you're not safe, Daddy. The people closest to you are the same ones who murdered some of your closest friends. And they're still here even though I showed you conclusive evidence of what they've done."

"No, princess. You showed me magic images that made it appear that they killed Margot. I need to examine the actual pictures to determine their veracity. And I need to interview Max, who produced them. Where are the images and where is Max?"

"I gave the picture machine back to Max, and I'm not certain precisely where he is right now. Have you checked his office?"

"Yes, we have. And he's not there."

They sit silently looking at each other for a couple of minutes. Then Rhylene stands and says, "So you're not going to arrest them or do anything to protect yourself from them?"

"Not until I can examine that device you showed me, look at the original images, and interview Max."

"I'm sorry to hear that, but I am glad you still seem to be safe. That's what I was wanting to know."

She stands and starts for the door.

"No, Rhylene. I don't think you understand what I'm saying."

The princess stops, turns, and looks at him.

"I need you to stay here with me until Max brings me that device with the pictures on it."

"I don't have either the device or Max."

"I know that—but you and Max seem to be rather close. I don't think he'll let you stay here under the control of Bynum and Carzikon if all he has to do to free you is to surrender that device with the pictures to me and answer some questions."

"You would imprison your own daughter?"

"Confining one's child to her quarters hardly constitutes imprisonment. Rather, it's a parent's prerogative—a form of discipline. Come with me."

He goes with Rhylene to her suite of rooms. Together they walk through them, examining each one carefully. He pulls out a chair, motions for her to sit, and says, "Have you reconsidered your position? Are you ready to do what I asked?"

"I can't, Daddy. As you can see for yourself, I don't have that picture device, and Max isn't here in my rooms. You're asking for what I don't have."

"Very well, Rhylene. You're confined to your quarters until you decide to be more cooperative."

He rises, walks to the door, and looks at the lock. Then he points at it, says something, and the door locks itself. He manually unlocks it, opens the door, and exits the room. He magically relocks the door, says something else, and a magical barrier forms across the door, which now appears to be encased in some unknown substance. He walks back to the king's office and sits down at his desk.

After watching both him and Carzikon for a few minutes, I tell Vicky to transport Rhylene while I walk outside to greet her.

"Did you see what happened?" she asks after materializing in Hidden Canyon.

"Yes, I did."

"I can't believe Daddy would do that to me!"

"That's because he's not your father."

"What? I realize he hasn't been acting quite normal recently, but I think I know my own father."

"Come with me and I'll show you," I say as I lead her to my office. Vicky plays the video of the man's transformation into King Kylandar. Rhylene makes me play it a second time . . . and a third. Then she sits in stunned silence.

"I can't believe it," she finally says. "Though that certainly explains a lot of things. For example, I was wondering when and where he learned the magic he used on the door to my room."

"It probably means we're dealing with a powerful wizard or magician who has taken your father's place."

"But where's Daddy? Is he still alive?"

"I'm sorry, Rhylene, but I don't know the answers to either of those questions."

"Is there some way to find out?"

"I don't know," I say before falling silent. After a couple of minutes, I add, "But I think I know where we might find one or more clues."

20.

When I took over Wizard Malmortiken's suite of rooms on the second floor of the palace, I discovered he had five large scrolls containing instructions and recipes for various magic potions and incantations. It's possible the recipe for the magic potion the strange man used to turn himself into the "spittin' image" (as my grandmother would say) of King Kylandar might be in one of those scrolls. If so, we might get one or more clues that could help us locate the king.

When I explain to Rhylene what I'm planning to do, she tries to insist on going with me, but I refuse.

"No. You won't be able to help me much there, but you might be able to provide valuable assistance by watching a live video feed from my office here. If I run into problems I can't handle, you can use your transceiver to give Vicky instructions that could save me."

"Okay, Vicky, transport me to my palace office," I say after walking past the waterfall in Hidden Canyon. The familiar tug on my midsection is replaced by the momentary cold feeling of nothingness. Then the walls and floor of my palace office materialize around me, and I find myself standing in front of my desk on the second floor of the palace.

I walk to the shelves that store Malmortiken's scrolls of magic and carefully pick up one of them, take it to the center of the room, and gently set it down. I repeat the action four times. When all five scrolls are lined up together, I place a circular disc on the middle of the center one and tell Vicky to transport them to Hidden Canyon.

Then I go to my desk, open the center drawer, and remove a divider. As I'm turning it over, I hear Rhylene's frantic voice in my transceiver.

"Max!"

"Yes? What is it?"

"Finish what you're doing and get out of there immediately."

"Why? What's happening?"

"They've discovered I'm not in my rooms on the third floor and are on their way down to your quarters."

I hastily pull out the magic wand that's hidden in the underside of the desk divider just as I hear the men approaching my door. Someone yanks on the door several times before being ordered out of the way. A word I don't recognize is exclaimed authoritatively and the locks open. Just as the doors spring apart, I feel my belly button being pulled into cold nothingness—and I land in the meadow of Hidden Canyon.

I pick up one of the scrolls, walk into the recess in the canyon walls behind the waterfall, and palm my way into my hidden quarters.

"Welcome back!" Rhylene exclaims as I enter my office and put down the scroll.

"Thanks—and thank you for getting me out of there in the nick of time."

"That was a bit close, wasn't it?"

"You can say that again."

"Is that the scroll we need to examine?"

"It's one of them. There are four more I need to bring in, and the others are just as big and heavy as this one."

"Why didn't you just transport them into your office here?"

"I can't. For security reasons, I designed these quarters so that folks can't transport directly in or out."

"I don't understand."

"As I've told you before, I'm not a wizard or magician, which means I don't fully understand how magic works. Since I don't want someone else to be able to beam into my home, I placed barriers all around to keep that from happening. But that also means I can't do it myself."

"Ah-ha! So that is why you always land us in the meadow, and we have to walk around the waterfall."

"That's right. Since my scanners are programmed to only recognize my fingerprints, I'm the only one who can open the doors and get us past the barriers that keep others out."

"I'll help you carry the scrolls."

We take the remaining scrolls from the meadow to my office, and then spend the next day and a half examining them. I'm working my way through the third one while Rhylene examines the fourth when she suddenly calls out, "Max! Look at this one and see what you think."

I sit down in front of the fourth scroll, look at the recipe she's pointing at, and begin reading the ingredients needed. "Powdered dragon wing, tail feathers of a skytan, shredded skin of a snortblast, sap from a guannaberry tree, powdered horn of a neuralank— Gag! Where and how do you get these things? And what in heaven's name is liquid essence of sommadunne?"

"Since we're not trying to actually *make* this potion, we don't need to *get* these items, Max. And liquid essence of sommadunne is a thick globular liquid found on the floating islands of Illa Dunne."

"Floating islands?"

"That's right. They seem to resist gravity. But those ingredients weren't what I was trying to show you."

"They aren't? You pointed to them, asked me to take a look, and tell you what I think."

"The part I wanted you to notice—and the part I find exciting—is that a necessary ingredient of the transformation potion is fresh blood from the person you wish to impersonate."

"Why does that excite you?"

"Don't you see, Max? *Fresh* blood. The recipe says the blood can't be more than three to seven days old, depending upon the temperature. That means Daddy has to still be alive."

"Oh . . .Ooohh. Yes. Of course. In order for his blood to be fresh. That may be the real reason Bynum is always leaving the palace."

"Max, that's it! Each time he returns from one of his trips, he comes back with a small case or satchel that he takes to the man who pretends to be Daddy."

"If the case contains transformation potion, he almost certainly got it from the place he went."

"And odds are that's where Daddy is."

"Bingo!"

"Bing what?"

"Bingo. In other words, I think that's the answer to where your father is."

She looks questioningly at me but doesn't say anything. I quickly change the topic by asking Vicky to show us where Bynum went. Vicky responds by lighting all three screens on the wall of my office. The middle one shows us a map of southern Ventryvia with a blinking arrow pointing at one spot. The ones on either side of the middle monitor show visual images from flying probes hovering near Bynum's destination. I lean forward and take a good look at them. They depict what appears to be a large country estate built on top of a hill.

"Vicky, get whatever probes are available into that building, including both some flying probes and some stealth probes."

21.

I lean back in my chair, think for a moment, and then say to Rhylene, "When I was getting Malmortiken's wand out of the desk, you contacted me and said they had discovered you weren't in your rooms on the third floor of the palace. What did they do?"

"They immediately left my quarters and headed for yours on the second floor."

"No, no. I mean what did they say or do about your not being there."

"I . . . I'm not sure. I was busy trying to warn you and get you out of there. I didn't really pay attention to any of that other."

"I see. All right. Vicky, show us what happened when the bad guys discovered that Rhylene wasn't in her quarters."

The map of southern Ventryvia disappears from the center screen and is replaced by an image of Kylandar's doppelgänger standing in the hall outside the door to Rhylene's suite of rooms. He says something and the magic barrier surrounding the door disappears. He opens the door and looks at the empty chair where the princess had been sitting.

The fake king enters the room, looks around, and motions to Carzikon to follow him. Carzikon steps into the room, holding a sword in attack position. They stealthily examine each of Rhylene's rooms, probing every place the princess could be hiding.

Nothing.

They search each of the rooms a second time. Still nothing.

The doppelgänger grunts an incomprehensible series of words and the walls turn blue. He studies each wall, turns to Carzikon, and says, "She didn't pass through any of the walls or windows. She somehow disappeared from the room itself."

He stands silently in Rhylene's bedroom for about thirty seconds, lost in thought. Then he looks up suddenly, locks eyes with Carzikon, snaps his fingers, and simply says, "Max!"

Carzikon's eyes widen, he nods in agreement, and both men rush from Rhylene's quarters. They go down the stairs to my rooms on the second floor.

Carzikon runs past the fake king and yanks on my door. It rattles but remains locked. He pulls on it repeatedly before being ordered out of the way by the fake king, who points his finger at the door, says something, and the lock clicks open.

Kylandar's doppelgänger pushes open the door just as I disappear when Vicky transports me back to Hidden Canyon.

"I saw him disappear from right here," the fake king says while standing where I had been seconds before.

"Max is obviously a more powerful wizard than we were led to believe. This could substantially change things. I should have eliminated him earlier but didn't think he was a threat. I won't make that mistake a second time."

They search each of my rooms before returning to the third floor. As they reach Fitzroy's desk, the king tells him to summon Premander K'Shay.

When K'Shay arrives, he is ushered into Kylandar's office.

"I sent for you because we may have a serious problem on our hands."

"What's that?"

"It appears that for the second time in as many years, I may have been betrayed by my wizard."

"Max?"

"Yes, Max. He's abducted my daughter, Princess Rhylene. I need you to alert your troops and arrest him on sight. This is a top priority for me."

"Are you certain she was abducted, Your Majesty? I mean—I often see them doing things together. Is it possible they simply went somewhere?"

"Possible, yes—but not likely. I had ordered him to come to my office. Instead, he vanished with her."

"Very well, Your Majesty. I'll put out an all-country order to find Max and arrest him on sight. What about Princess Rhylene?"

"Rescue her and return her to me."

K'Shay leaves the room, and the video screen fades to black. "Wow," I exclaim while leaning back in my chair. "So now I'm a wanted man."

"Isn't it great to be wanted?" Rhylene asks, flashing a half grin at me. "But shame on you for abducting me like that."

I roll my eyes and shake my head at her. "Seriously, Rhylene, this will make it much harder for us to search for your father."

Her face becomes somber as she replies, "Yes, I know. And it was already hard enough. What especially worries me is his talk about how he should have eliminated you."

"Yeah. That's troubling to me, too. But it doesn't change the fact that we've got to find your father."

"No, you're right," Rhylene agreed. "If anything, it makes it even more imperative."

22.

"There are three doors on the ground floor plus another one on the second floor," I tell Rhylene as we look at pictures of the estate we think might contain the real King Kylandar. "The right screen shows a live feed from the carrier probe that's transporting smaller probes we'll try to get inside the building."

"Why isn't it in color like the other visuals?" Rhylene asks.

"Because it's a live picture from a flying probe taken in total darkness."

"Isn't the screen on the left also showing live visuals?"

"Yes, but it's from a camera mounted on a stationary tripod. And its camera has a larger lens."

"And that makes a difference?"

"Yes. Trust me; it does."

We watch the flying carrier probe landing near the back door and unloading several smaller probes. It then goes to the door on the second floor and repeats the procedure.

A few minutes later Vicky reports, "All probes appear to be working properly. Now it's just a matter of getting them inside."

"Good job, Vicky. Let us know when you get them in."

"Will do."

I turn to Rhylene and say, "It may take a while to get them inside. In the meantime, let's get something to eat."

While we're eating, Vicky contacts me on my transceiver. "I'm sorry, sir, but I am unable to get any of the probes into the building."

"Not even the smallest ones?"

"No, sir. Each of the doors has barriers that seal the openings, probably to keep bugs out—but they are also effective in keeping out our probes."

"What about the other doors?"

"I sent small flying probes carrying a couple of stealth probes to both of them, but none of them could get past the barriers."

"Well, drat! Thanks for trying, Vicky. Keep the stealth probes right next to the doors. Maybe we can get some in when a door is opened."

I sit back in my chair, look at Rhylene, and tell her what Vicky said.

She asks, "Is there any other way of getting your probes inside?"

"I suppose I could physically take some. Go in disguise, pretend to be a peddler or something. If I can get inside, I may be able to drop some off."

Rhylene says, "I could go instead. They haven't issued an arrest warrant for me—at least, not yet."

"No. You're better known across the land—more likely to be recognized. The people in this estate have never seen me before. I should be safe. Well, safe enough, anyway. Besides, if you and Vicky are watching, you should be able to get me out of there if things go bad."

We brainstorm for a while about various items I could attempt to peddle but are unable to agree upon anything having even a remote chance of success. I finally suggest going as a troubadour.

"I worked my way across Ventryvia last year as Finaro's assistant," I remind Rhylene. "I can probably do some of the same routines I did then. I still have my costume and some of the musical instruments I used."

She reluctantly agrees.

We wait until we see Bynum mount his sorrak and ride away. Then Vicky beams me to a clearing near the country estate, and I walk from there.

I knock on the front door. And wait.

Nothing.

I knock again, somewhat louder. This time I hear a woman's voice yelling, "Jenny, answer the door."

I hear footsteps approaching, and the door is opened by an attractive young black-haired woman who is about five and a half feet tall. She stares at me briefly before asking, "Whatcha want?"

"Please excuse me," I respond, "but I'm working my way across the land doing odd jobs or entertaining people in exchange for food."

"Wait there and I'll ask," she says before closing the door.

As I'm waiting, I hear hoofbeats approaching. I turn around and see Bynum riding back toward the house. *Oh, rats! He may recognize me!*

I say a silent prayer that the girl hurries back before Bynum gets there. She does, but it's with the message that they're not interested.

As she starts to close the door, she sees Bynum and hesitates. He walks up onto the porch, places a hand on my shoulder, and asks, "What's with you?"

"I'm working my way across the land doing odd jobs or entertaining people in exchange for food," I repeat without looking directly at him.

He studies me for a moment or two, nods and says, "Yeah, I think I may have something for ya. C'mon in." He points to a couch and says, "Have a seat." He walks into another room, and I'm left alone.

I quickly reach into my coat pockets, remove the stealth probes, and toss them under the couch.

"C'mon in here," Bynum says to me while pointing toward an adjoining room. I get up, and as I walk past him, he slaps me on the back of my neck.

I realize it's more than just a slap when I feel the sting of a needle shortly before passing out.

23.

When I come to, my body is aching, and I feel disoriented. My head seems to be spinning. I'm locked in a cell, and my left leg is chained to boards that serve as my bed.

What time is it? I look at my left wrist, but my watch is gone. I check my ears. My transceiver is missing, which means I can't communicate with either Rhylene or Vicky. Not good.

Not good at all.

But then again, even if I could communicate with them, I'm not sure they could transport me out of here if my leg is chained to a steadfast object.

After a few hours, the girl I'd met at the door brings me some soupy stew. I don't know whether it's safe to eat—but since I'm famished, I taste it carefully, savor it momentarily, and then wolf it down. They could have already killed me if they wanted to do so. The girl says her name is Jenny and she's a slave girl. She won't say who her master is or what he does.

After she leaves, Bynum comes to my cell, holds up my transceiver, and asks what it is.

"Hearing aid," I lie. "I don't hear real good out of this ear," I say, pointing to my left ear. I hope he'll give it back to me, but he doesn't.

"The king wants to know why you abducted his daughter."

"I didn't."

"He says you did. Says he'd confined her to her room, but you magicked her outta there."

"What gave him that idea?"

"He saw you do the same thing to yourself a little later."

"Doesn't mean I abducted her. Why did you attack me?"

"I'll ask the questions. Why're you snooping around here?"

"I like to roam around the country, meeting people. I hadn't been here before. That's all. No harm in that, is there?"

"You're not 'specially good at lying. Ya know that?"

I don't answer. Just look at him. After we stare at each other for a few minutes, he leaves.

Bynum returns later. I'm not sure how long it's been. Might be the next day. I'm still a bit disoriented. He grabs me, lifts me up like a rag doll, and shakes me while growling, "We need ya to tell us how you magicked yerself and the princess outta the palace and where ya went."

I mutter, "I don't know what you're talking about."

"Don't give me that," he yells, slamming me against the bars of the cell. He punches me in the gut, slaps my head around, and then picks me up a second time and crushes my face against the bars.

"Does the king know you're doing this?" I gasp.

"What difference does it make?"

"Just listen and think for a moment."

Bynum pauses in his beating, though he appears ready to continue.

"The king reinstated Haughton as his butler and promoted K'Shay to be commander of his army."

"Yeah. So?"

"Both betrayed the king less than a year ago, but he brought them back. Said he wanted to heal divisions. So how much sense does it make for you to beat up his friends while he's reconciling former enemies?"

Bynum just holds me in midair while his mind attempts to comprehend what I've just said. The logic of my message eventually seeps through, as he relaxes his hold on me and sets me down on the boards forming my bed. He grunts, turns, and leaves the cell without saying anything else.

24.

Time drags by. During the next several days and nights, I see and hear no one other than the slave girl, who brings me food and water. The real King Kylandar is apparently not imprisoned near my cell, since I can find no signs of him.

I'm awakened from a solid sleep by a gentle nudge. I open my eyes and am startled to see Rhylene unlocking my chains.

"Shhh," she cautions. "I've gotta get you outta here."

"How did—"

"Shhh. Don't talk. Just follow me."

She quietly leads me up two flights of stairs, through the kitchen, and out a back door. A full moon lights our way as we run down a path, through an area filled with trees, and into the woods behind the house, where two sorraks are tied.

She hands me a small slab of beef and a hip flask containing water. "Maybe this'll help a bit," she says.

"Why don't you just transport us?" I ask.

"What?"

"Contact Vicky using your transceiver—you know, your earpiece—and tell Vicky to transport us."

"Oh, yeah; the earpiece. Sorry. Lost it. We'll just have to use sorraks."

I nod and we both mount. We ride about fifteen minutes before coming to a larger road that takes us to a village I don't recognize in the darkness. However, the town is at an intersection between the road we're on and a larger road that Rhylene says goes from Nantanna to Trojhalter.

We ride all night, arriving at a cliff overlooking Trojhalter shortly after dawn. The city is built on an island in the Argondola River and is reached by a bridge from the southeast side of the river. A smaller bridge spans the Argondola to the east for travelers from the north.

Since the city gates are opened at sunrise, we are able to join a good number of farmers and merchants making their way into the city. We don't want to be recognized, so we pull our hoods over our heads. We nevertheless hang back until the soldiers at the gate are busy inspecting a fully loaded cart being driven by a surly man who's arguing with the soldiers. Then I nod to Rhylene and we casually move by on our sorraks.

The smell of rotting garbage reminds me that we're in Trojhalter, where people dump their refuse out open windows into the streets. A pack of creatures resembling some kind of cross between dogs and monkeys is ravaging a large pile of garbage we have to go around, and several of the beasts growl at us as we pass.

"What are you looking for?" Rhylene asks.

"I have a friend who works here as a blacksmith. He may be able to help us."

She nods, and we continue along the dusty streets until we reach Horace's shop. We dismount outside the large swinging doors, lead our sorraks inside, and close the doors behind us. We both remove our bags from our sorraks.

"My gods! Is it actually Max?" exclaims a big burly man with a black beard, who looks up from his forge and anvil.

"I'm afraid so, Horace," I reply, and reach out to shake his hand. "I don't know whether you've met Princess Rhylene."

"I've only seen ya at a distance—and a considerable one at that," the blacksmith says, bowing slightly. The princess smiles graciously at him. "What brings ya this way?"

"Do you still have your transceiver?" I ask.

"Yeah. Do ya need it back?"

"No, but I need to borrow it momentarily. We've been through a scrape, and we both lost ours."

"Sure thing," Horace replies, removing a transceiver from his left ear and handing it to me.

I speak into the transceiver while holding it with both hands. "Activate. Vicky, can you hear me?"

"Yes, sir."

"Do you have Rhylene and my coordinates, so you can transport us to Hidden Canyon?"

"You mean where you are now?"

"Yes."

"I have the transceiver's coordinates. Place it first on yourself and then on her."

I do as Vicky instructs before returning the device to Horace and thanking him.

A sudden pull on my midsection confirms that Vicky is transporting me. I pass through the cold void and land in the grassy meadow of Hidden Canyon. Happy to be home, I look at the princess and notice her terror-stricken eyes.

"Are you still not accustomed to being transported?" I ask.

"I don't know if I'll ever get accustomed to it," she replies.

We walk around the lake and waterfall, I palm the controls to allow our entrance into our quarters, go to the kitchen, and fix us a pizza. While it's hydrating and cooking, I turn to the princess and say, "All right, Rhylene. Tell me what happened."

"What do you mean?"

"They knocked me out with some drug, chained me to a board bed in a cell, beat me up, and interrogated me. After a few days and nights, I wake up to discover you are busy rescuing me. That's all I know. I need you to fill in the details."

"Well," Rhylene says while drawing a deep breath. "I'll try, but I don't really know all the details." She pauses, collecting her thoughts. "You disappeared after going into that house, and I couldn't reach you. I knew I had to do something but didn't know what.

"I finally disguised myself as a scullery maid, went to the stable behind the house where they keep the sorraks, and made friends with the stable boy. He introduced me to the slave girl who works in the house, I gave them both some money, and they agreed to help me.

"She gave me the keys I used on your cell and chains, we borrowed two sorraks, and I think you pretty well know the rest." Rhylene looks at me and shrugs. "I guess that's about it."

"Remarkable!" I exclaim. "Thank you."

"You're most welcome. Were you able to find out anything?"

"Not really—other than your father isn't imprisoned in the same cells where I was kept. I wasn't able to find him."

We eat our pizza and then go down the hall to my office. I replace our lost transceivers and have Vicky bring up visuals of the country estate. While I was languishing in my cell, Vicky has moved the stealth probes into several rooms inside the house. Although none of them show Kylandar, Vicky informs me that six of them are in rooms Bynum may have gone to after disappearing.

Vicky also shows me a computer-assisted design layout of most of the first floor of the house. The ten rooms the probes have explored are depicted in white, while the unexplored areas (based upon the outside dimensions of the house) are blue.

I tell Rhylene, "You and I escaped up two flights of stairs before going through the kitchen. Do you remember where the stairs are?"

"Let me get my bearings," she says while studying the diagram. She points to a room and says, "The kitchen is right here . . . We came from this direction, so the stairs should be over here somewhere," and she points to a blue area to the left.

"Thanks," I tell her. "It's getting late. I'm tired. Why don't we both go to bed and take this up again tomorrow."

"What do you want to do?" she asks nervously.

"Just go on to your bedroom, and I'll see you tomorrow."

She looks tense, fidgets a bit, and then asks, "Would you go with me? After all we've been through these past few days, I'm nervous about going anywhere alone."

I look at her a bit strangely, but mutter, "All . . . right. After all you've done for me, I'll be glad to accompany you."

The princess smiles up at me, latches hold of my arm, and we stroll through the halls to her room.

"Would you please check the room to make sure we're alone?" she asks.

I explore the room with her, but everything looks the same to me as before. I tell her good night and then walk down the hallway toward my bedroom. As I do, I hear the lock click on Rhylene's door.

"Vicky," I say into my transceiver. "Have you disabled both of the transceivers we lost?"

"Yes, sir."

"Could you fill me in on the details of how they were lost?"

"Yes sir. Yours was taken from you after you passed out from the drug Bynum injected into you. They removed everything from your pockets and then found the transceiver in your left ear. I turned off its speaker but left on its microphone and tracker so that we can continue obtaining information. Rhylene spent her first night there in the stable. As she told you, she tried making friends with the stable boy, and he let her sleep in one of the stalls. However, during the night he heard her talking to me. He surprised her and took the transceiver away from her. I'm not sure what he did with it, but it stopped working. Consequently, I lost contact with both of you until you made your escape."

"Thanks, Vicky. Keep moving the stealth probes to areas where we can obtain the most information. We've got to find Kylandar—and I don't know how much time we have."

"Yes, sir."

After locking my own bedroom door, I slip out of my clothes, take a nice hot shower, and get ready for bed. I read a couple of chapters in my Bible and do my normal nocturnal devotionals, quiet time, and prayer.

I pull back the covers, crawl into bed, but can't go to sleep. Instead, my mind keeps reviewing the events of the past few days.

I feel certain King Kylandar is imprisoned somewhere in the house where I was also a prisoner. But where?

I never heard his voice, though I think I may have heard cell doors clanging shut somewhere—but it was far enough away that I can't be sure. If that's what I heard, I'm pretty sure it's on a different floor from where I was locked up. Well, Vicky will be trying to get probes throughout that house. If he's there, we'll find him.

I close my eyes but am still unable to sleep. What's bothering me, anyway?

My thoughts keep going back to Princess Rhylene. The way she held on to my arm as we walked to her bedroom was almost exactly the way Becky held me before she died back on Earth. And that's not all. I'm suddenly remembering how Rhylene's body felt when I grabbed hold of it at the farview device. Instead of pulling away or getting mad, she flashed a mischievous grin and said, "Kinda startling the first time, isn't it?" Maybe she was referring to more than just the castle walls appearing to fall away. Or maybe not.

Still, she's awakened feelings I thought were dormant. I didn't think anyone besides Becky could ever make me feel this way. And the way she looked at me then—and several times since then, for that matter—reminds me of the way Becky used to look at me.

Oh, Becky! How I miss you, Darling!

When you were killed in that automobile accident, part of me died, too. Or at least I thought it had. That's why I took this mission to a far-away planet. I've travelled this many light years away from Earth—but the memories and longings are still with me, threatening to engulf me.

Becky had cinnamon hair and eyes, while Rhylene's hair is more of a cinnamon-auburn shade, and her eyes are a silvery blue. But both girls are beautiful with small, perfect features. Both have radiant skin and soft supple bodies with graceful feminine curves. Both have an air of self-confidence, dazzling smiles, and a quirky way of lifting one eyebrow when amused. In short, Rhylene looks, feels and sounds so much like the wife I buried back on Earth that I find myself longing to be cuddled up by her side, holding her close to me.

Snap out of it, boy! You're probably old enough to be her uncle. Yeah, but that's calendar years. While I was coming to this planet, I was in hiber-sleep travelling at the speed of light. I hardly aged at all.

And what about the bits of affection she's shown? Well, what about them? It's all right for her to have some affection for a friend or uncle. But even favorite uncles aren't there to put moves on the girl or to try to cuddle her in any way. That would come out of the blue like some kind of shattering, psychologically damaging betrayal.

There's also the fact that she's a princess and I'm a commoner. And then of course there's the really BIG ONE: I'm an alien from a different planet. So, no matter how much she reminds me of Becky, there can be no future for us together. Not now. Not ever.

So it's better if I think of her as a friend or niece rather than as a potential lover or my missing wife. Yeah, better. But still not easy when I'm suddenly aware of feelings and emotions that must remain dormant and suppressed.

25.

After getting dressed the next morning, I wander down to Rhylene's room. Her door is closed, and I decide not to disturb her. *Let her sleep, since she can use the rest.* I go to my office, put in the security codes, and ask Vicky if there have been any developments overnight.

"Yes, sir. You need to look at this."

Vicky turns on the center screen on my wall, and I see the man who is pretending to be Kylandar sitting at his desk. He responds to a beeping noise by opening a desk drawer and taking out a mirror about six to eight inches in diameter. He touches a button on the handle and the beeping stops.

He looks into the mirror and says, "Yes. What is it?"

A feminine voice responds, "Sir, I'm reporting as ordered."

"Yes, Jenny. Go ahead."

"Max has access to powerful magic, but I'm not sure he's the one actually doing it."

"What do you mean?"

"He's working with a powerful sorceress or witch named Vicky who seems to be the one who actually performs the magic."

"Tell me more."

"He uses that earpiece to contact Vicky. Since neither of us had our earpieces, we had to ride sorraks all the way to Trojhalter, where he borrowed an earpiece from a friend of his. Once he got in touch with Vicky, she magicked both of us to some kind of house he's built in a canyon somewhere."

"How long did it take you to get from Trojhalter to the canyon?"

"Not long at all. Just a few moments. Just long enough to scare me to death."

"What do you mean?"

"Everything went black, I felt a tugging at my midsection, and I felt this horrible cold surrounding me, pulling me into a void. But before I could scream, we were in a canyon meadow near a waterfall. Then we walked to Max's place, which is carved out of solid rock. I've never seen anything like it."

"But it was this witch or sorceress who actually moved you there?"

"Yes, sir."

"What does she look like?"

"I never saw her. I only heard her voice—and not very well, since she was talking to Max through his earpiece."

"You mean she was able to perform her magic without even being physically present?"

"That's right."

"That *is* powerful magic."

"And that's not all. She can also produce magic pictures of some of the rooms in the house where King Kylandar is being kept."

"Which rooms?"

"Just the ones at the front of the first floor so far, but she's trying to see into the others."

"So she hasn't found our captives?"

"Not yet. Whoops! Gotta go. I hear Max coming down the hall."

"Good report, Jenny. Keep me posted on everything."

"Yes, sir."

The fake king sits holding the mirror for several moments before putting it back into the drawer. I sit for a similar amount of time, thinking about what I've just seen and heard. *The girl who "rescued" me isn't Princess Rhylene. The real princess has been captured and is being held prisoner—apparently in that house where I was also a prisoner. The slave girl impersonating Rhylene will probably know where they are. But will she tell me? Even if she does, how will I know whether she's telling the truth?*

After mulling this over for a few minutes, I ask Vicky to contact Finaro, the troubadour I worked with when I first came to Ventryvia. After a few minutes, Vicky reports, "I'm unable to reach Finaro. His transceiver is working and is turned on, but he's not answering. He's probably not wearing it."

"How am I supposed to contact him if he doesn't even wear it?" I grumble.

"You haven't talked with him in months. He probably didn't see any point in continuing to wear it."

"Good point, Vicky. All right, contact Jamistan."

A few seconds later I hear static, which is quickly replaced by a man's voice saying, "This is Jamistan."

"Hello, Jamistan. This is Max. I'm trying to reach Finaro, but he's not wearing his transceiver. Do you know where he is?"

"Sure do. He's right across the table from me. We're eating breakfast. Do you want to speak to him?"

"Absolutely."

"All right. Here, Finaro. Max wants to talk with you," and I hear the transceiver being handed over to him.

"Finaro here."

"Would you be willing to come back to Hidden Canyon for at least an hour or two while I question someone?"

"I suppose so, but why do you want me there?"

"If I remember correctly, your special magical talent is being able to discern whether a person is telling the truth. Is that right?"

"Yes."

"I need to interview someone, and I must know when she's truthful and when she's lying."

"Very well. When do you need me?"

"Right now, if possible."

"All right. I guess I'm ready—or will be as soon as I return this earpiece to Jamiston."

"Stay in the same spot where you are while wearing the transceiver."

While Vicky transports Finaro, I walk outside to greet him.

"Welcome back to Hidden Canyon, Finaro. I have reason to believe that a girl named Jenny is impersonating Princess Rhylene. I think she has taken a transformation potion that allows her to look and sound just like the real Rhylene."

"Transformation? Is that even possible?"

"Unfortunately, yes."

We walk back into my quarters and are met by Rhylene's doppelgänger.

"You remember Finaro, don't you?" I ask.

"Uh . . . sure," she responds.

I glance at Finaro, and he shakes his head slightly.

"Let's go into my office and see if we can figure out where the bad guys are keeping King Kylandar," I suggest while leading the way. "Vicky, show us the layout of the country estate building."

It appears on the center screen. I turn to the fake princess and say, "Now, I need you to show us where Kylandar is being kept."

"I—I don't know where he is."

Again Finaro shakes his head.

"On the contrary: I think you do know, **Jenny**."

"No, I—I—Why'd you call me that?"

"Isn't that your name?"

"No. Of course not. You know who I am. After all we've been through together, how can you even pretend to not know me?"

"Isn't Jenny the name you used when you contacted your master with your report about me?"

"I don't know what you're talking about."

"Then let me refresh your memory. Vicky, show us the video."

As the girl watches and listens to the video, her eyes widen in surprise, wonder and fear—and then fill with tears. Slumping in her chair, she wipes her eyes and asks, "What is it you want?"

"The truth. Actually, I want several things. Let's start with something I think I already know—but I want your answer anyway. Why did you set me free?"

"My master wants to know more about you. When you disappeared from the palace, he realized he'd underestimated you and the magic power you possess. He wasn't able to answer his questions by merely capturing you or having Bynum beat you up. When we caught Rhylene, he commanded me to use the transformation potion to become her and take her place, rescue you, accompany you while helping you escape, and report back to him what I learn."

"That's what I thought," I reply. "What I'm especially interested in is saving the lives of two very dear friends of mine who are being held captive by your master and his associates. As far as I'm concerned, that trumps everything else. I think you know where they are, and I need your help."

"I'd like to help you; I really would. But if Jonnasloan finds out I helped you, he'll kill me. Or worse."

Finaro gives an affirmative nod.

"Who's Jonnasloan?" I ask.

"He's my master—and he's also the man who's pretending to be King Kylandar."

"Does he have any magical or special way of tracking you?"

"I don't know. He's a powerful sorcerer—so he might."

"Tell me more about him."

"When he first bought me as his slave, he was just a man—a man obsessed with obtaining power—but nevertheless, just a man—and at his core, a rather good man. He hadn't yet sold out to the forces of evil. He was simply a lawyer who desperately wanted to win a case he was handling."

"How desperately?"

"Enough to make a deal with demonic forces."

"You mean he sold his soul to the Devil?"

"No. He was too sharp a lawyer to do something *that* dumb, but he made some kind of deal that allowed him to win a frivolous case. I don't know what he had to do or give up at the outset, but it was enough to allow demonic forces to get a hook into him. He's been getting more deeply involved—and consequently more evil—as his power has grown."

"You say he was just a lawyer at first?"

"That's right. A hard-working lawyer who tried to do a good job for his clients. But he let his priorities get out of order. It got to where the ends justified the means."

"What do you mean?"

"Instead of doing the best job he could for his clients within the law and code of ethics, he became obsessed with winning at any cost. Winning became his measuring stick of whether he had done a good job.

"And Jonnasloan is a good enough lawyer that he almost always won his court cases. But he would go into a deep depression whenever he lost. It was during one of those periods that he met Count DeVil."

"Who's that?"

"That's what the man called himself. I think he's either the Dark Prince of Abaddon or is someone awfully close to the Dark Prince. Anyway, they started off as acquaintances and then became friends. As their friendship blossomed, Jonnasloan's power and prestige grew—and he slipped further and further away from all that is good, proper, and ethical. His moral compass was compromised. But what pushed him over the edge was the Doe case."

"Doe? Like John Doe?"

"Who's that?"

"Never mind. Like a female deer?"

"Yeah, but it was the guy's name. He came to Jonnasloan with a real tear jerker of a tale that totally appalled my master."

"What kind of story?"

"He claimed his daughter had been sexually abused by the child's teachers at a private school. Doe embellished the tale with all sorts of lurid details that captivated my master's attention. It was almost like magic. Jonnasloan was outraged at the injustice and took the case, certain he could win a huge award for Doe—with a hefty sum for his own attorney's fees as a nice bonus.

"The case became an obsession to Jonnasloan, and he devoted almost his full time to it. But he became frustrated at the lack of evidence supporting Doe's claims. Doe had been so good at telling his story that he had beguiled Jonnasloan, who was convinced his client was telling the truth rather than seeing him for the con man he actually was.

"Jonnasloan eventually turned to Count DeVil, who said he could help him win his case, including the large jury award he had dreamed about. They worked out some kind of deal—I'm not sure exactly what—but Bynum and his wife eventually came to live with Jonnasloan."

"What's Bynum's connection?"

"He works for DeVil or is an associate or something. Together they introduced Jonnasloan to the power of magic, and he became obsessed with it and the power it could give him. He brought home books of magic, various artifacts, and other unusual objects. He put a lock on the door to the basement, and he'd vanish down there for hours at a time. Some nights he wouldn't even go to bed.

"Strange things started happening. Objects would lift up and float around the room. Drapes sometimes caught on fire and burned to a crisp. Other times they might catch on fire but not be harmed. He could point at a door, and it would close and lock itself.

"Practicing magic took progressively more and more of his time, and practicing law took less and less. He eventually closed his office and turned exclusively to magic. That's when Count DeVil came to him with another proposition. I don't know what they agreed upon, but it was shortly after that when he moved all of us to the country estate you visited."

"You mean the place where I was captured before you set me free?"

"Yes."

"Where did Jonnasloan get the transformation potion?"

"Bynum's wife is a witch who knows how to make it. He regularly comes back to the house to be with her and to get more potion."

"Is that where Kylandar and Rhylene are?"

"Yes."

"Will you show me where they are?"

"I don't know. If I do, Jonnasloan and the others will know—and I'm as good as dead."

"I'll do my best to protect you."

"Nothing personal, Max, but your best won't be good enough. Jonnasloan has the power of Abaddon behind him."

"Abaddon? You mean the power of Hell itself?"

"That's one of the names it's called. The one Jonnasloan uses is Abaddon. But yes, that's the power he can call upon."

"Wow! Well, you're right. That's definitely more power than either King Kylandar or I possess. Unless, of course, God himself chooses to intervene."

"But you don't have any guarantee your god will."

"No, I don't."

"And therein lies my problem. I'd like to help you but dare not betray my master."

I glance at Finaro, who gives me an affirmative nod.

"Jonnasloan doesn't know where we are right now, does he?"

"No. At least, I don't think he does."

"Show me on the layout of the house where Kylandar and Rhylene are, and maybe I can rescue them. Jonnasloan will still have possession of the palace, but my friends will at least be away from that place of evil without your having to go there or otherwise be personally involved. You've already told him that we have ways of seeing what's in the house and are trying to see more—and that's without any assistance from you. If you want to go back to your master, I won't stop you—but you also would be welcome to stay with us, and I'll try to protect you."

Jenny's eyes again fill with tears. She wipes them and sits still for a moment while thinking. Then she rises and walks to the screen depicting the first floor of the house.

"The stairs are located here," and she points to a spot to the left of rooms shown in white. "They are in the basement, which is one floor below this room right here," and she points to the living room. "You were in the sub-basement, almost directly below them."

Finaro again gives an affirmative nod.

"Vicky," I say into my transceiver, "I need to see those rooms."

"Yes, sir."

I turn to Jenny and say, "Show me your magic mirror."

She momentarily acts startled, but then rises and leads me to her bedroom. Jenny rummages around under her bed, pulls out a pouch she had earlier carried in her saddlebag, and opens it. She grabs a mass of scarves, unwraps them, and removes a hand mirror.

"This is a mirror that has been enchanted to allow scrying and messaging."

"How does it work?" I ask.

"If I merely want to see what someone I know is doing, I tell the mirror to scry him. If I want to talk to the other person, I tell the mirror to scrymarron him. This mirror will send a signal to that person's enchanted mirror, causing it to beep. When he turns on his mirror, we can see and talk with each other."

"May I try it?"

"Certainly."

I take the mirror and tell it to scry Rhylene. Instead of showing me Rhylene's doppelgänger, who is standing next to me, it shows the real princess, sitting on her bed inside a jail cell.

"I can't talk with her unless she also has an enchanted mirror, right?"

"Not just an enchanted mirror. It must be the same enchantment as your mirror in order for it to work."

"Thank you," I say while returning the mirror to Jenny. "Now give me your flasks containing the transformation potion."

Jenny sighs, reaches back into her pouch, and withdraws a hip flask.

"There's this one," she says, handing it to me. Then she pulls up her skirt and unhooks another flask from a leg holster while continuing, "and this one. They're both the same."

I open one of the flasks, stick in a glass rod, and say, "Analyze."

A few minutes later, Vicky reports back to me. "It appears to be the same potion as the one in your formula—except it has Rhylene's blood added to the other ingredients, of course."

26.

While we're eating lasagna in the kitchen, Vicky buzzes me on my transceiver and says, "I've found them!"

I get up, go to my office, and look at the live feed Vicky is providing. Kylandar and Rhylene are in adjoining cells. The king is shackled to his bed similarly to the way I was, but his daughter does not appear to be chained to anything.

As I watch, she stands up, walks to the bars separating her father from her, and begins quietly talking to him.

"Rhylene appears to be unshackled," I say into my transceiver. "As soon as you have her coordinates, transport her here."

As we watch, the picture shifts as the probe moves to a point directly over Rhylene, and then continues to shift as it drops down, moving from her head to her feet and back up again.

"Got it!" Vicky exclaims. "I'm transporting now, and then will get coordinates for Kylandar's cell. I'll transport you next."

"Let me welcome Rhylene first."

I turn to Jenny and say, "Come with me."

We walk toward the meadow and meet Rhylene coming around the waterfall. Rhylene does a double take as she sees her doppelgänger.

"Who's that?" she demands.

"Welcome, Rhylene," I say. "I think you've met Jenny."

"Hummph! She said she was going to help me free you—but I got locked up instead."

"Actually, she did help free both of us. I'll tell you all about it when I return."

"Where are you going?"

"I've got to free your father before the bad guys discover you're gone. Keep an eye on things until I get back. Finaro can entertain you until then."

"Finaro? He's here too?"

"Yep. I'll explain that as well when I return. All right, Vicky; I'm ready."

The red canyon walls disappear into the cold black void and are replaced by a dungeon cell containing my friend, King Kylandar.

He looks up at me and says, "I was hoping Rhylene's disappearance meant that you were rescuing us."

"I've got her, Your Majesty, and I hope I can get you as well. But we have to break those chains before trying to transport you out of here."

I change the setting on my blaster to laser, kneel beside Kylandar, and pull the trigger. The blaster emits a steady light stream that cuts into the iron chain binding the king to his bed. I am focusing so intently on cutting the chain without injuring Kylandar that I tune out everything else—until I'm brought back to reality when he suddenly whispers, "Max! Hide!"

I freeze and glance up in time to see the stable boy entering the cell block from the stairs. He doesn't initially see me kneeling beside Kylandar, and I crouch closer to the king, attempting to hide under the boards forming Kylandar's bed. The king drops his blanket over me, smiles at the boy, and says, "What have you got, boy?"

"Just some soup, sir."

"Thank you, son. Just put it under the door and I'll get it."

The stable boy pushes a bowl under the bars, stands back up and moves to Rhylene's cell.

"Hey! Where is she?" he asks.

Kylandar replies, "I think they took her upstairs for questioning."

"I didn't see her. Who took her?"

"I don't know. I've been asleep and didn't see."

"I'll need to check on this."

"Fine, son. You do that."

The boy puts down the second bowl of soup and races out.

I quickly get out from under the blanket, turn the laser back on, and continue cutting. Just as the chain breaks apart, I hear several people coming down the stairs.

"Vicky, get us out of here quickly!" I say into my transceiver while huddling next to the king.

The boy runs back into the cell block room, followed by Tybatha and someone I don't recognize. The witch's eyes widen in alarm when she sees me next to the king. She raises her hands and starts shouting some spell just as we are transported into the void.

As the canyon walls of home materialize around us, Kylandar and I fall into a tight embrace while gasping, "That was close."

"Welcome home, Your Majesty."

"Thank you, Max—for everything. Rhylene has filled me in on your attempts to find me. The last she heard, they had captured you as well. How did you get free?"

"Come on inside and we can talk."

27.

"Oh, Daddy!" Rhylene squeals, running and embracing him. "It's so good to have you back."

"Thanks, honey. It's great to be back. I've been so—"

Kylandar's words break off as he catches sight of a second Princess Rhylene, this one seated sedately at the kitchen eating bar. His eyes dart back and forth between the two, comparing them.

"What is going on?" The king's voice has a sharp edge to it.

I point to the second princess. "This is Jenny, the slave girl who brought you food while you were a captive—unless she and your daughter decided to fool us by switching places."

I watch the girls' reactions.

"No, I'm the real Princess Rhylene," says the one who had embraced Kylandar.

"And I'm actually Jenny, as you should be able to clearly see when the potion wears off, which it should do fairly soon."

"What potion?" the king asks.

"Transformation potion, Your Majesty," I say. "That's why your captors kept taking your blood, which is a necessary ingredient. "They used that potion to impersonate you and Rhylene. Come into my office and I'll show you."

I play the video of Jonnasloan transforming himself into the image of King Kylandar.

"That's remarkable!" he exclaims. "He now looks and sounds enough like me that it even fooled my own daughter. But why is he doing it?"

"You're the king of Ventryvia," I answer. "I presume Jonnasloan at least wants your power as ruler of the land. Jenny, what else?"

We turn and look at the slave girl.

"My master made some kind of bargain with the Dark Prince of Abaddon. I don't know all the details, though I do know parts of it and can probably guess most of the rest."

"You mean he sold his soul to Evil?" Kylandar asks.

"No, not yet. If he had lost his soul, he would be fully under demonic control. I think he merely is providing the demons with a way to escape from Abaddon."

"Escape?" asks Kylandar. "I thought that was their home."

"It is—but it's also their prison. They are confined there and want a way out, which a willing ruler might be able to provide."

"Why would any sane ruler willingly allow demons to roam his land?"

"An army of demons is a formidable force. My master craves power. He's smart and crafty. If he can negotiate something that gives him what he wants without giving up too much in the bargain, he's likely to expand his covenant with the Dark Prince of Abaddon."

"Heaven help us!" I exclaim, and the others turn and stare at me. I grimace and shrug.

"Although he currently possesses the throne of Ventryvia," Jenny continues, "it is by impersonating you, Your Majesty." She nods at Kylandar. "Since you are no longer their captive, their supply of your fresh blood will soon expire. Once that happens, they can no longer make their transformation potion, which means Jonnasloan will no longer be able to pretend that he's you."

"What do you think he will do?" I ask.

"Whatever it takes to maintain his power. If he can no longer keep the throne by impersonating King Kylandar, he'll do it some other way—any other way—even if it means making an enhanced deal with the Dark Prince."

"Then I've got to confront him immediately," Kylandar exclaims. He turns to me and asks, "How quickly can you get me back to Van Seissling?"

"What are you planning to do?" I ask.

"Take back my throne, of course. You can vouch for me when we meet N'Shawn, and he can lead the Dragon Company up to my chambers in the palace. If we need more men, we can use the King's Regiment. They'll be loyal to me."

"Uh, Sire," I stammer, "The King's Regiment and the Dragon Company aren't in Van Seissling now, and N'Shawn no longer commands your army."

"What?"

"Yes, Your Majesty. Jonnasloan moved all of them to Trojhalter and put Premander K'Shay in charge of your armed forces."

Kylandar drops into a chair, shakes his head, and says, "This may be harder than I had imagined."

"Yes, Sire," I agree. "It undoubtedly will be."

28.

"Hello, master."

"Yes, Jenny. What do you wish to report?"

"Max has rescued both King Kylandar and Rhylene."

"Yes, Tybatha just informed me on her enchanted mirror. That means they know you're not Princess Rhylene."

"Yes, sir. They know, but they haven't locked me up. I may be able to escape if that's what you want me to do. They think that since I'm your slave, I won't want to return to you—so they are allowing me to stay here if I choose to do so. What do you want me to do?"

"Do you know where you are?"

"No, sir. I have no idea."

"So you probably couldn't make your way back even if you did escape."

"Probably not, sir."

"Very well. Stay there. Watch and listen. It'll be helpful to have an informant inside their base of operations."

"Yes, master."

Jenny terminates the transmission, turns off the enchanted mirror, and hands it to me. I carry it into my office and lock it inside my safe. Then I return to the kitchen table where Jenny has joined the others.

"Your master has now been notified and has given his permission for you to remain here," I say to Jenny. "That should lessen the danger to you in the event he defeats us and remains king of Ventryvia. On the other hand, if you help us and we are successful in restoring Kylandar to the throne, we'll set you free and you will no longer be a slave."

Kylandar leans forward, touches Jenny on her wrist, and pledges, "If you work with us and help me reclaim Ventryvia, I'll personally see to it."

Jenny tears up again, bites her lip, and mumbles, "Thank you."

29.

Since Kylandar has asked to talk privately with Rhylene and me, the three of us have gathered in my office. The door is closed and locked. Jenny's still in her room, while Finaro is eating something In the kitchen.

Looking at his daughter, Kylandar says, "When we were locked in adjacent cells, you told me some of what has happened since I left with Yarrod to go hunting. I want to know more."

"What parts do you know?" Rhylene asks.

"I remember everything up until I went to sleep at my hunting cabin. I woke to discover I was tied up and gagged inside a wagon. Men I'd never seen before carried me into a house and down some stairs to a jail cell in some sort of dungeon. I was chained to my bed, though the chain was long enough to let me sit on the chamber pot in my cell.

"They brought me food and water, and periodically drew blood from my arms. I don't know how many days that went on, but Rhylene was stuck into the adjoining cell after a considerable period of time. She told me you had also been captured," and he nods in my direction.

"At that point, I began to seriously question whether we would ever get free, since all three of us were captives. Yet here we are, free—though I'm no longer on the throne."

"So you were asleep when you were captured, right?" I ask.

"That's correct."

"And you didn't see who captured you?"

"No, not when it happened, though I presume they were the same ones who were driving the wagon and who later carried me into the house."

I have Vicky play the video we'd saved of the wagon being driven down the highway toward Nantanna. Even after Vicky enhances the images, we are initially unable to identify the man driving the wagon. Of course, much of the problem is that the view of the man and wagon are from overhead. We can see the top of his head, but not his facial features.

Vicky freezes the image of the man on the right screen and then plays the video of Jonnasloan, Haughton, Bynum and Carzikon riding to Van Seissling on sorraks. A shot from high overhead provides a good comparison of images.

"This one right here looks like the same man as the guy driving the wagon," Kylandar says.

"I agree, Your Majesty," I add.

"Yes," says Rhylene. "That definitely helps identify the driver as Bynum."

"So Bynum was involved in both murders," I note.

"Murders!" exclaims Kylandar. "What murders?"

Rhylene glances at me and grimaces. Her dad didn't know his friends had been killed. She quietly says, "We found Yarrod dead outside the hunting cabin, and later Bynum and Haughton went to Margot's house and killed her."

"Haughton?" asks Kylandar. "You mean my old butler murdered the sweet old lady who was almost my second mother?"

"Well," I reply. "I think Bynum actually did the killing, but Haughton took him to the house."

"Killing a harmless old couple like Yarrod and Margot is unforgiveable," Kylandar fumes. "What else have they done?"

Rhylene answers, "You already know about the transformation potion Jonnasloan used to take your place as king. Since your blood couldn't be more than a few days old, Bynum had to keep going back and forth between the palace and that country estate where you were imprisoned—but that's how we were able to discover where you were."

"Yeah," I add, "but unfortunately, we were unable to get any of my probes into the building, which is why I had to physically take them there."

"And that's when they captured you," Kylandar says.

"Yep. That's when they got me. You pretty well know the rest, since Rhylene has filled you in regarding her capture."

"Right," says Kylandar. "Since they no longer have access to my blood, what will they do now?"

Before either Rhylene or I can answer, Vicky announces, "We may be about to find out."

"Why?" asks Kylandar. "What's happening?"

"Bynum and his wife are passing through the outer gates of Van Seissling." Vicky responds while posting new video on the screens mounted on one wall, which show various views of Bynum and Tybatha riding through the streets of Van Seissling.

They pass through the inner wall of the city, ride to the royal stables, and dismount. Leaving their sorraks at the stables, they go past the security guards outside the palace, and enter the building. Different probes pick them up and transmit pictures of them walking up the stairs to King Kylandar's office on the third floor.

Bynum introduces his wife to Fitzroy, who welcomes them both and announces their presence to Carzikon. That aide immediately ushers them into Kylandar's office, where they are welcomed by Jonnasloan.

"These are the last bottles of potion we can make," Bynum tells Jonnasloan, and hands him three hip flasks. "The two silver flasks contain the king's potion, while the black one is his daughter's."

"Understood," Jonnasloan says. "You two can go on in to my sitting room and relax while I put our plan in motion."

He walks to the door to the king's private office, opens it, and tells Carzikon, "Summon Premander K'Shay. Tell him to come to my office immediately."

Jonnasloan puts one of the silver hip flasks into his coat pocket and places the other one into a desk drawer. Then he sits back and waits.

About ten minutes later, Carzikon returns with K'Shay. The military commander waits at Fitzroy's desk while Carzikon announces him to Jonnasloan, who takes a deep sip from a hip flask and immediately begins transforming into King Kylandar's doppelgänger. When the change is complete, K'Shay is ushered into the room.

The fake king stands and returns his commander's salute.

"At ease, Premander. Immediately after breakfast tomorrow morning, I want you to assemble the troops under your command on the parade grounds just outside the inner wall of Van Seissling. I have an important announcement I want to make to them and to the people of Ventryvia."

"Yes, Sire. Do you want all the troops, or should I leave the ones guarding the walls, gates and dungeons?"

"Leave those but assemble everyone else."

"Yes, Sire. Immediately after breakfast tomorrow morning. It shall be as you ordered."

"Thank you, premander. You're dismissed."

Premander K'Shay stands, salutes, and marches from the room.

We watch for a few minutes with no one speaking. Then Kylandar clears his throat and drawls, "Well, it looks as if we shouldn't have to wait much longer to find out what my imitator has planned."

"Yep," I agree. "Tomorrow morning—or sooner. Vicky will notify us if there are any more developments before then."

"If we launch an attack on Jonnasloan and his minions, who can we count on to be with us?"

I think momentarily before answering, "If you talk to N'Shawn and we show him the videos we have, I'm pretty sure he'll answer your call."

"And of course there's those of us here," Rhylene adds.

"Which side will Jenny be on?" Kylandar asks.

"Ask her," I say. "Finaro's magic talent is telling whether someone is being truthful—so ask her in his presence."

"I want my kingdom back—" Kylandar broke off what he was about to say, stood defiantly and said, "I *will* have my kingdom back. The forces of evil shall be punished and heads will roll for what they did to Yarrod and Margot. Are both of you with me on this?"

Rhylene and I both nod our heads. Then I add, "Yes, Your Majesty. They crossed some lines that shouldn't have been crossed."

30.

We have an early breakfast the next morning, and then gather in my office to view the proceedings on my video screens. We watch Haughton bring several trays of food up to King Kylandar's office, followed by the co-conspirators eating heartily. The right-hand screen on my office wall, which is displaying a view of the parade grounds, merely shows a few street sweepers cleaning the area to make it ready for the announced assembly of troops. A few dozen people begin gathering around the outside perimeter, and troops begin marching onto the parade grounds and forming up.

Jonnasloan stands, turns to Bynum and Tybatha, and asks, "Any last questions or comments?"

"No," Bynum answers, while his wife merely shakes her head.

"All right then; Let's do this."

He hands Bynum the two silver hip flasks, and gives the black one to Tybatha. They each open a flask and drink deeply. Bynum immediately begins transforming into the person of King Kylandar, while his wife becomes Princess Rhylene. After the transformations are complete, Jonnasloan hands Bynum Kylandar's royal robe and crown, and Bynum puts them on. He helps Tybatha put on one of Rhylene's travelling coats. All three co-conspirators examine themselves in a mirror.

They leave the king's private office and move into the hallway on the third floor of the palace. Cameras from various probes record their progress as they step down the stairs, out the palace, and onto the viewing area atop the inner wall of Van Seissling.

Bynum—now transformed to appear as King Kylandar—moves regally to the podium at the center of the viewing area, looks over the troops gathered below on the parade grounds, and nods to K'Shay. The premander commands, "Parade rest!"

The soldiers move from attention to parade rest and turn their heads toward the person pretending to be their king. Thousands of private citizens crowd into the plazas surrounding the parade grounds.

Bynum holds his hands out, symbolically asking for silence. When the crowds quieten, he speaks in King Kylandar's voice, amplified via magical enhancement.

"Five years ago I asked you to join me, my wife, and Wizard Malmortiken as we formed an alliance to defeat the powerful criminal warlords who had ruled this land for centuries. Together we were successful in reclaiming Ventryvia and ending many of the abuses that had plagued our country for too long. Together we have made great progress, though there is still work that must be done. It hasn't been easy, and there have been setbacks—chief among them being my wife's death two years ago and the rebellion led by my wizard last year.

"Nevertheless, we have successfully completed the major goals I had when I first asked for your support. The next phase of our development can best be achieved if Ventryvia is led by someone who is an administrator rather than a warrior. After a long and diligent search, I firmly believe I have found the right man to lead us on to greater achievements."

Kylandar's doppelgänger turns toward Jonnasloan and says, "Come here, my friend. Let me introduce you to the people."

Putting his arm around the other man, Bynum turns back to the crowd and declares, "This is Jonnasloan, a man I believe is perfectly suited to lead Ventryvia to greater heights than could be done by anyone else, including me. Give him your allegiance and your support."

The fake king then removes his royal crown and holds it high above his head for all the crowd to see. Turning toward Jonnasloan, he places the crown firmly on his head. Kylandar's doppelgänger kneels before the new king and calls out, "Long live King Jonnasloan." The crowd below takes up the chant—rather hesitantly at first but growing louder and more confident with each repetition.

*****

The real King Kylandar sighs while watching the proceedings on my video screens. Then he grimaces and says, "Well, it appears—both to me and to anyone watching this scripted play—that I have just abdicated my throne and turned the kingdom over to Jonnasloan."

"What can we do about it?" I ask.

"I don't see that we have any choice but to oppose him. I fear for the safety of the people of this land. Any man who is so power mad that he'll murder harmless old people like Yarrod and Margot and make deals with the Prince of Abaddon and his demons, is totally unfit to be king. He's dangerous. We've got to do something."

"But what?" asks Rhylene.

"Let's brainstorm for ideas," answers her father. Turning to Jenny he asks, "Are you with us or against us?"

"I'm with you."

I glance at Finaro and he gives an affirmative nod.

"You understand the odds we're facing here?" Kylandar asks Jenny.

"Probably better than anyone else in this room," she responds.

"Do you pledge to be loyal to me and not to sell us out to your master or any of his minions?"

"I do."

"Why?"

Jenny seems shocked by the question, but quickly recovers. "As long as my master is in league with evil, he's not fit to lead the people. I think there's still good in him, but I'm afraid that whatever good that remains will be buried forever unless he and the Dark Prince can be stopped—and you're probably the only one who can do that. But don't ask me how because I don't know."

"Jenny," I say softly. "You told me earlier that Jonnasloan bought you on a slave auction block. What did you do before that?"

"My parents died several years ago, and I was given a place to live by an uncle who had a small farm. I worked for him until he died. His children let me continue working there while his estate was being settled. But eventually they sold the farm and I had to leave.

"I wandered from place to place, doing odd jobs as best I could—maid, servant, slopping pigs, cook's assistant, and so forth. Anything I could do for a meal and a place to sleep."

"A vagabond," I suggest.

She looks at me curiously and asks, "A what?"

"Uh, a wanderer; a person without a fixed residence or home."

"Yeah, that's right; a wanderer. But what was the word you used that means wanderer?"

"Vagabond."

"Vag-a-bond. Vaga-bond. Oooh yeah, I like the sound of that. Anyway, I was working as a cook's assistant in Trojhalter when some ruffians captured me and then sold me on their auction block as a slave."

"That's not fair," Rhylene says.

"Since when has fairness determined anything that really matters in this world? Anyway, Jonnasloan bought me—which was fortunate, since he used me as his maid and servant rather than what a lot of men use young girls for. It definitely could have been worse."

"Jenny's not the only vagabond here," Kylandar says.

"What do you mean?" I ask.

"Since Rhylene and I have been ousted from the palace, we also have no fixed place of residence or home—so we also qualify as being vagabonds."

I look at him without saying anything, but I silently remind myself that since I'm the only one present who is not from this planet, I may be the biggest wanderer of all.

When I visit with Finaro later, he says, "My magic talent tells me that Jenny told us the truth—at least to the extent of what she said."

"What do you mean?"

"She's not telling us everything about her relationship with Jonnasloan. She's hiding something."

31.

"Sir," Vicky says through my transceiver, "Please go to your office and turn on your screens. I need to show you something."

When I comply, an image is projected onto my middle screen that looks vaguely familiar.

"Is that Lake Zaragon?" I ask.

"It is."

"I thought so. It's hard to forget the spot where I almost died. I would have if you hadn't rescued me by blowing up Wizard Malmortiken's tower."

"Yes, sir. You're looking at the island where his tower had been."

"Why is there so much smoke coming out of the ground?"

"That's not smoke, sir."

"What is it?"

"A thick cloud of some kind of creatures swarming out of the hole in the ground where the wizard's tower was before we destroyed it."

"What kind of creatures?"

"I don't know, sir. I've been unable to find anything like it in my memory banks."

"How many probes do we have around Lake Zaragon?"

"I moved in twelve flying probes to monitor Wizard Malmortiken before your battle with him. Five are still in the area."

"Keep monitoring the Wizard's Island with one or two probes, but let the others keep an eye on the swarm and watch wherever the creatures go. Record their movements and actions—and get more probes into the area around Wizard's Island."

"Yes, sir."

I tell the others and they come into my office to watch the spectacle.

"Are there caverns under that island?" I ask. "Could those be bats?"

"Bats normally come out at dusk," Kylandar responds. "It's close to midday. Also, I don't remember anything like either the hole or these swarms when we were there last year."

"You're right on both counts," I say while trying to remember what the island looked like just after the tower was destroyed. "If I recall correctly, that island was just barely large enough to hold Malmortiken's tower. It appears to have grown since then."

"Perhaps the water level of the lake has dropped some," Kylandar suggests.

"Maybe."

"It reminds me of swarms of bees or locusts."

"True—but I've never seen any bees or locusts that are as large as these things. Or which sound like these."

"Yeah, how would you describe it? Sort of a loud metallic buzz?"

"Yes, Your Majesty. Something like that."

Vicky interrupts, "Whatever the creatures are, they have just attacked a farmer. I'm putting it on your right monitor."

That screen comes on, and we shift our gaze to it. We watch video from a probe that's obviously flying along with the swarm of creatures. Part of the swarm peels off from the main cloud and flies toward a farmer's house in the midst of his fields. A lone man is near the door to the house.

Several of the creatures fly around the man, and at least one of them lands on him and stings him. He lets out an agonized yell, falls to the ground, and begins rolling in the dirt, writhing, screaming, thrashing, slapping at his legs, and trying to cover his face.

A second man runs out from the house holding a large wooden paddle that he swings back and forth, swatting at the creatures. He grabs the first man, lifts him up, and carries him into the house.

"What in the world!" I exclaim.

"I don't know," answers Kylandar, "but it's not anything good."

"That's for sure. Vicky, can we get a closer look at any of those creatures?"

"I'll try," Vicky answers. "The second man hit one of them with his club. It appears to be at least stunned. Let's see—"

The video picture suddenly shifts back toward the ground, where one of the little animals lies motionless. We watch as the camera zooms in on it.

The creature is several inches long with a body that mostly resembles a cicada, since it is segmented with insect-like legs. Its rear portion consists of a large scorpion-like stinger tail that's reddish pink in color.

Its face is similar to a man's except it's much more grotesque. It's red beady eyes glare with malevolence and evil desire. It has teeth that protrude from its mouth like the pictures I've seen of prehistoric saber-toothed tigers. It's hard for me to believe that so much ugliness can be packed into so small a space. The revulsion I feel is almost enough to make me vomit.

As we watch, the creature stirs, rises and flies off to rejoin the others. Our probe follows, gradually overtaking the swarm of mutant cicada-scorpions.

Vicky's voice crackles in my transceiver, "Sir, I'm turning on your left screen to show you a different swarm."

"Different? Where's this one coming from?"

"It originated at the same place—Wizard's Island on Lake Zaragon—but earlier than the swarm you've been watching. When the creatures first appeared, the wind was from a different direction—so this swarm initially went southwest instead of east. I assigned some of the flying probes to accompany it."

"Thank you for doing that, Vicky."

The left monitor shows a smaller cloud of cicada-scorpions flying over a river. Vast grasslands extend to the right and another river is on the horizon—right on the other side of a city located near the confluence of the two rivers.

"Where is this?" I ask.

"They're going southeast near the Andora River gorge," Vicky answers. "They are approaching the city of Korivan, and the river on the far side of Korivan is the Argondola."

As the swarm flies over the outer wall of Korivan, individual cicada-scorpions break off from the main swarm and begin attacking people on the ground. One of the creatures lands on a woman's neck. She screams and clutches at her throat as a man next to her reaches over and pulls the bug off. It stings him, and he drops to the ground, writhing in pain.

We watch as dozens of people are attacked. Those who are stung appear to be largely incapacitated, while the people who are merely bitten continue to fight back. One man is able to tear the wings off one of the creatures before being stung. The cicada-scorpion falls to the ground, where it is stomped by another man wearing work boots. A third man wraps a thick cloth around the bug, scoops it up, and puts it into a small cage. It fights its way out of the cloth but is unable to escape from the cage. Its humanesque face is livid with fury, but its captor seems only concerned with making the cage more secure.

"Wow!" Jenny mutters.

"What is it?" I ask.

"That creature was just stomped into the ground—but all that stomping didn't seem to faze it except to make it even angrier."

"By golly! You're right. The only damage it sustained was having its wings ripped off."

I think for a moment before speaking. "Vicky, don't you have additional flying probes in Korivan?"

"Yes, sir. I have probes throughout Ventryvia to assist our communication and data collection, and they are more numerous in populated areas such as Korivan."

"Keep some of the probes in the areas where people have been attacked by those creatures. We need to know whether they recover."

32.

"Sire," says Fitzroy while knocking on the door to King Jonnasloan's office. "Premander K'Shay and a royzan from Korivan say they need to see you immediately about some kind of emergency."

Since he was no longer pretending to be Kylandar, Jonnasloan no longer required Carzikon to intercept all visitors in order to give him more time to transform himself.

"Show them in," Jonnasloan commands.

The two military commanders salute their king. He returns the salute and motions for them to be seated.

"Fitzroy said you wish to report an emergency."

"Yes, sire," says K'Shay. Motioning to the other man, he continues, "This is Royzan L'Nara from Korivan. His commander, Manatar K'Starna, sent him here to report directly to you."

Jonnasloan turns to L'Nara. "All right, soldier. What do you have to report?"

"Korivan has been invaded by a swarm of flying beasts that bite and sting people of the city."

"Flying beasts? How big are they and what are they like?"

"They're about the size of a man's hand and have a huge stinger similar to a scorpion's. I don't know whether their stings are fatal, but they are at least extremely painful. My commanding officer dispatched me immediately to report the attack to you."

"Do you know where they came from?"

"No, sire. A swarm of them just appeared this morning. I initially thought it was a cloud of locusts or other insects. But they're worse than anything I've ever seen before."

A knock interrupts their discussion.

"See who's at the door," Jonnasloan says to K'Shay, who does as he is told.

When he opens the door, Fitzroy sticks his head in to tell the king, "Sire, two more men are here from Korivan, and they've brought some unusual animals for you to see."

"Show them in."

A man wearing a dark green jacket enters the room holding a box or package of some sort covered with a tarp. Accompanying him is a man in a military uniform who apparently is serving as his escort.

"Sire," he says to the king, "My name is Arvin, and I've captured a couple of the beasts that attacked Korivan earlier today. May I show you?"

"By all means."

Arvin carefully removes the tarp from around the cage, which holds two of the cicada-scorpions. One of them is the wingless one we saw earlier, while the other one's wings are still intact, though they appear to have been beaten up or bent.

Jonnasloan gets down close to the cage and carefully studies the creatures.

"I've never seen anything like them!" he exclaims.

"Nor have I, Your Majesty," says K'Shay. The others make similar comments.

The wingless beast grabs hold of wires forming the outside of its cage and turns its hideous face toward the men in the room, studying them closely. Although its scorpion-like stinger continues to pulsate threateningly, the rest of its body remains motionless, which allows Vicky to get good closeup pictures of it from one of our probes in the room.

The central portion of its body has three pairs of legs and is similar in appearance to a large cicada. The front pair grasps the cage much as a man might hold on to something with his hands. Its body is segmented with alternating bands colored brown and yellow with a few black areas.

The rear of the animal consists of a huge yellowish-brown scorpion-type stinger that is translucent enough to see venom sloshing around on the inside.

Perhaps even more hideous is the creature's face, which is shaped enough like a human's to make its features appear even more loathsome and evil. Its red beady eyes look hungrily at the people in the room, and it has several sets of teeth—one in front of another—which are constantly in motion. It reminds me of a bat or shark going mad in a feeding frenzy. The teeth in front, which are out of proportion to the rest of the face, have long canines like those of a lion, the upper pair extending over the lower lip. I had earlier noticed the two large teeth extending outside the mouth, which reminded me of prehistoric saber-toothed tigers. Now that I can study them more closely, I think they may be more like the fangs of venomous snakes.

Growing out of the top of its head is long reddish-brown hair, flowing like a woman's, spilling out from under a golden protrusion which looks like a small crown or partial helmet. Thus, the creature combines human features with those of insects and anthropods. It is hard, compact, and nearly invincible.

"What is it?" Jonnasloan asks softly.

As if answering the question, the creature responds with noises that almost sound like human speech saying, "A bad one! A bad one!"

I turn from watching the screen when I hear a gagging sound from Kylandar. His face has suddenly drained of color.

"That's what I was afraid of," he mutters.

"What do you mean?"

"It's saying 'Abaddon.'"

33.

As I pour myself another cup of sorrinaugh, I briefly consider how remarkable it might seem that I have finally found some brew I actually like better than the coffee to which I was addicted back on Earth. Although I sometimes miss some of the flavors that were available for coffee, sorrinaugh makes a wonderful substitute.

I sit back down in the chair behind my desk and ask Kylandar, "So what can you tell us about Abaddon?"

"Abaddon is the legendary place of demons," he answers. "Or at least I always thought it was merely legendary. Now I'm not so sure."

"What do the legends say?"

"Some say it's a place of the dead, while others claim it's a bottomless pit where demons, devils and other evil creatures are confined."

"If its bottomless, couldn't the creatures escape through the place the bottom would otherwise be?"

"Bottomless means it goes on forever."

"That's illogical."

"Maybe, but that's what the legends claim."

Jenny leans forward and says, "You're thinking of a three-dimensional physical object, Max. Instead, try to envision a supernatural object in a spiritual dimension."

"You mean a dimension that transcends those of our physical universe?"

"I'm not sure I understand what you're saying, but I think you may be on the right track."

I briefly consider this before turning back to Kylandar. "Sorry to have sidetracked the discussion. You said it's where demons and other evil creatures are confined. What else?"

"Just that it's supposed to be a place of destruction and damnation. Quite frankly, I never gave it much thought. But those creatures we saw are very real."

"Yeah," I agree. "Even if they appear to be left over from nightmares. What caused them to appear now?"

"It would be too much of a coincidence for it not to be connected with Jonnasloan's taking the throne. Jenny, what do you have to say about it?"

The slave girl shifts uncomfortably in her chair before answering. "I know Jonnasloan was making some kind of deal with the Dark Prince of Abaddon, but don't know any of the terms other than my master wanted to be king, and the Dark Prince wanted an exit point from Abaddon for his demons. It appears they both got at least those objectives."

"Who is this Dark Prince?" I ask.

"I'm not sure other than he's apparently in charge of the underworld. He may be the same person or demon as the Count DeVil who helped my master several times or it might be someone else entirely—but I'm pretty sure there's some connection between them."

"Sir," Vicky says. "Sorry to interrupt, but there's something I think I should show you."

"Go ahead."

"While you've been brainstorming, I've been monitoring Jonnasloan and the things going on in his office. The soldiers and others from Korivan have left, and he has used an enchanted mirror to contact Count DeVil. I recorded their conversation and am putting it on your right monitor."

"Thank you, Vicky."

When the screen comes on, we see Jonnasloan sitting at his desk, looking intently into a mirror he's holding tightly and saying, "This is NOT what I agreed to."

"Nonsense!" replies a smooth masculine voice from the mirror. "It's precisely what we agreed upon."

"I only agreed upon an exit point for your demons to leave Abaddon. They were not supposed to attack anyone or anything. I specifically required that they leave Ventryvia."

"And they have left Ventryvia."

"Yeah, but they attacked numerous people first—and those people are my subjects. I never agreed to *that!*"

"I can't help it that the wind was blowing the wrong direction at first. I don't control the wind. Besides, the demons you're complaining about have been cooped up for many years. When they finally got loose, it's only natural they'll feed on any tasty morsel they fly over. Don't get so upset. I gave you what you wanted, didn't I? You're king—so enjoy the power and prestige."

"But your demons attacked some of my subjects—

"That's twice you've mentioned *your subjects*." The Count paused and then laughed, "You make it sound as if you're the legitimate king. Don't take everything so seriously—and don't forget that I'm the one who put you in power and gave you what you wanted."

"But I only agreed that some poor creatures that had been unfairly imprisoned in an underground dungeon could be set free. I didn't give them permission to attack anyone. I didn't even know they'd be demons until after we'd reached initial agreement and Kylandar had been captured."

"You had a minor emergency you hadn't expected. That goes with the territory of being king. Consider it a learning experience. If you feel you must blame someone, blame whoever it is that controls the wind. Is there any other reason you called me?"

"Uh—yes, there is. Bynum murdered an elderly couple needlessly. Why did—"

"It wasn't needlessly. They were in the way and had to be eliminated."

"They were a harmless old couple. There was no reason for—"

"I said there was sufficient reason. People and things that get in our way are simply eliminated. It's easier and more efficient that way. Do you understand what I'm telling you?"

"But—"

"Do you understand?"

Several seconds of silence pass before Count DeVil rasps in a voice so devoid of warmth that it sounds practically frozen, *"Do. You. Understand?"*

"Uh . . . yes."

"Good! And don't contact me again about anything as unimportant as this."

The Count apparently has terminated the conversation, since Jonnasloan sits uncomfortably staring at the enchanted mirror for several minutes before slumping forward in his chair. He eventually opens a drawer in his desk, places the mirror inside, and then continues to sit with his head in his hands.

The room reverberates with the sound of raucous laughter coming from the two caged demons.

.

34.

"So Jonnasloan apparently didn't order the killing of Yarrod and Margot," Rhylene says as I refill her cup.

"Yeah," I agree while hydrating a seafood pasta dish. "Jenny may be right about there still being some good in him."

I glance at Jenny just in time to see her wipe a smirk from her face.

"But is there enough good there for him to actually oppose the demons he's allied himself with?" I ask her.

"I—I really don't know," she stammers. "I desperately want to believe there is, but—"

The statement is left hanging, unfinished.

"For what it's worth," Kylandar says after a moment, "I didn't see him at the time I was captured."

"You didn't?" I ask.

"No. He may have been a part of it, but I didn't see him. Bynum was driving the wagon I was in, and Carzikon helped him carry me into the house where I was imprisoned. There may have been some others, but I — I don't remember any of the actual event. I must have been asleep or passed out or something."

"The wine you drank was drugged," I say while serving the food I'd cooked.

"I suspected something like that had happened. When I woke up, I was tied up inside a covered wagon being driven by Bynum. I didn't know Yarrod had been killed until after you rescued me."

35.

Jonnasloan sits at his desk thinking about his conversation with Count DeVil. The change in DeVil's attitude has shaken Jonnasloan to the core. Always before, the Count had been gracious, pleasant and easy going. And he was this time, too—at first.

But when I pressed my complaint about the demons attacking my subjects, he got defensive and took the side of the demons. And when I brought up the killings of that elderly couple, he got downright belligerent. Even sinister and threatening.

What was it he said? He warned me that "People and things that get in our way are simply eliminated. It's easier and more efficient that way." Then he asked if I understood what he was telling me.

The thought of what DeVil said and the way he said it terrorizes Jonnasloan, and his body shudders as he thinks over the warning Count DeVil has given him about what could—and probably would—happen to *him* if he gets in the way of DeVil or his demons. He slowly rises to his feet and shuffles to the balcony outside his office, where he gazes absent-mindedly at the courtyard below. Putting his hands on the parapet, he mutters to himself, "How did I get myself into this mess, anyway?"

He remembers, of course. Indeed, the memories sometimes haunt his dreams at night. Like many practitioners of the law, he is well aware of problems, inequities and injustices present in the legal system. He wasn't above taking advantage of shortcomings or loopholes when it could benefit either him or a client, but it still bothered him.

But what could he do? He wasn't the one who made the laws. That was the king's job. So he gnashed his teeth and fretted in silence—or griped about it with friends or other lawyers.

Then he met Count DeVil. The Count had helped him win a case he despaired of ever being able to win. To this day he didn't know how DeVil had done it. Truth be told, he didn't really want to know. But the two men had become good friends after that, and he had come to believe that the Count could help him achieve even his fondest, most far-fetched dreams.

Jonnasloan confided in DeVil. Told him his hopes and dreams and listened to the Count's replies and assurances. One of the things he revealed was that he wished he were the king so that he could do away with the unjust and unfair aspects of the law.

DeVil responded by introducing Jonnasloan to the world of magic and showing him some of the astounding things that could be accomplished using magic and sorcery. But magic also has its limitations, boundaries, and senseless rules. For example, DeVil said he had long wanted to free some poor helpless creatures that had been magically imprisoned in an underground dungeon—but only the king or supreme ruler of the land could allow it to be done. Alas, neither of them was king.

But the seed had been planted. As the two men worked together on various projects—some legal, some magical, and some that were neither—the seed germinated and quietly grew until Jonnasloan agreed that if DeVil would help him become king of Ventryvia, he would give legal permission for the Count to free the poor creatures that had been imprisoned in the dungeon.

But now Jonnasloan knows that the creatures are not helpless, and there is a very good reason they had been imprisoned. Even worse is the knowledge that they are evil demons, his "friend" is their lord and master, and Jonnasloan is now threatened with being eliminated if he gets in their way. A lot of good it does him to wear the crown! Jonnasloan now realizes that while he might officially be king, the supreme ruler is actually Count DeVil.

36.

"Please excuse me," Vicky says in my transceiver, "but I've been monitoring some events in and around Korivan you should probably see."

"Vicky wants to show us something that's happening in Korivan," I tell the others. "Bring your plates to my office; we can eat in there."

"I've recorded several things for you to watch," Vicky says over the office speakers. "The first one is of a man who was injured after being stung by demons outside Korivan."

When the center screen comes on, we see a man seated on a rock overlooking a river. He's drinking something out of a bottle, and a similar empty bottle is on the ground next to his right foot. He's being recorded by one of the flying probes that has been accompanying a swarm of demons.

As we watch the video recording, we see three of the demons in front of the probe leave the main swarm, zoom down to the man, land on him, and begin stinging him. He swats at the creatures, jumps off the rock, and tries to run from them—but is not coordinated enough to do so. Instead, he falls into a deep ravine and just lies there, twitching uncontrollably.

Vicky explains, "Since I had other probes with the swarm, I ordered this probe to stay with the man. I was afraid he may need medical attention, and we'd need the probe's coordinates to find him again. But notice the change that starts to occur within a few hours. I'm skipping forward four hours in time."

Although the man appears to be unconscious, his body is convulsing while shrinking and changing color. His clothes sag and appear much looser on him, and his face is changing shape, becoming less human and more ape-like.

"This is what he looks like now," Vicky says as the image changes. The man's body and clothes are still in the same place and position as before, but his image has changed to something resembling a large dark purplish chimpanzee wearing the man's clothes.

"Is that the same man?" I gasp.

"Yes. That's why I am showing you this image first—so you will understand the origins of the creatures you will see in the other recordings I'm about to show you."

The first picture fades from view and is replaced by a video of a monkey that's running through the streets of a city. Mist is seeping through the streets and crannies between buildings, which is not especially unusual for towns like Korivan that are close to rivers. But this mist is exceptionally thick, and tendrils of it drift through hedges and around stones. Vicky freezes the picture, moving it forward one frame at a time until reaching a particularly good view of the creature so we can study it more closely.

Since it isn't wearing any clothes, we can see that it's more ape-like than human. It lacks the hairy body of most apes, but that might just be because it hasn't had much time to grow body hair. It has dark purple skin with deep walnut-brown highlights, but the skin is crinkled and shriveled. It's back is arched like that of a cornered cat, and its face is distorted and maddened, cheeks hollow, nose flattened to almost nothing, with a sharp and narrow chin. A pair of small black wings has sprouted on its back between the shoulder blades, though they appear too small to be useful for flying.

"Are you ready for me to continue the video?" Vicky asks.

I glance at the others, and they nod affirmatively.

"Go ahead," I say.

When the video goes back in motion, we see that the monkey is chasing a group of human children. It pauses just long enough to grab feces from between its legs and throw it at the children. The feces only goes a few feet before spontaneously bursting into flame. One of the children sees it coming, yells a warning to the others, and they scatter away from the incoming flaming mass, which hits a nearby house and sets it on fire.

As the children round a corner, they are confronted with three more monkeys heading their way. Behind the apes are several more burning houses.

The children quickly change direction again, this time running toward some soldiers who appear to be responding to the emergency.

The monkeys stop long enough to reach between their legs for more feces, which they hurl at the soldiers. Although the sight of flaming excrement seems to startle the military men, they are battle hardened and don't panic. Instead, they raise their shields to block the fireballs and continue advancing toward the monkeys.

The apes look and chitter at each other, giving us a view of their needle-sharp teeth and long protruding tongues, and then they hurry back the way the single monkey had come while chasing the children. About halfway down the block they skitter to a stop as another squad of soldiers comes into view.

One of the men raises a bow and shoots an arrow at the nearest ape. The monkey lets out an agonized scream as the arrow passes through his abdomen, and then collapses as a second arrow pierces his heart.

The three remaining monkeys throw flaming excrement at the door of a nearby house. When the door catches fire, they pick up the dead ape and try to use him as a battering ram against the burning door. Although they're eventually successful, the door holds long enough for an archer to pick off a second monkey. The other two race through the fire and into the house.

The ranking officer issues commands to the two squads, posting one outside the house and sending the other one into the structure. Our probe stays outside—but since we don't see the monkeys anymore, we can't tell what happened to them.

Instead, Vicky shows us additional scenes from around Korivan. Fires—probably caused by flaming feces—burn in various parts of the city. Hundreds of monkeys have managed to seize control of one small section of Korivan, where they are making a successful stand against the soldiers in that area.

Military archers position themselves on any high points they can find that command unobstructed views of the sector overrun by the mutant monkeys, and periodically succeed in picking off a stray. However, the creatures use their flaming excrement to set new fires—especially around concentrations of soldiers.

Since none of the combatants pay attention to our flying probes, several of them are able to mingle with the mutants—which allows us to continue studying them. They no longer appear to be human. Rather, they now are manifestations of evil, reflections of the monsters to which they have fallen prey.

Noticing something different about them, I ask, "Is it my imagination, or have the creatures changed their appearance?"

"What do you mean?" Kylandar asks.

"I don't remember their backs being black—but now they are."

"By the beard of Zorkus, you're right! What's happened to them?"

Rhylene answers, "I think their wings have been growing. They were tiny, but now fully cover their backs."

As we watch, one of the monkeys soars haltingly into the air, where he is immediately shot down by several archers. The creatures on the ground gather as a group and chatter among themselves for a minute or so.

Then the entire mass of mutants take positions as near to the archers as they safely can, reach between their legs for more ammunition, and then hurl it at the soldiers. The incoming missiles ignite en route.

It's more than the archers can handle. Facing and deflecting individual wads of flaming feces is one thing. But hundreds of them? Forget it!

The soldiers break into full-scale retreat, tripping over each other in their haste to race down any available stairs or ladders while trying to get away from the wall of fire that hungrily devours the places they had been—and where some of their comrades perished in the flames.

Having rid themselves of the threat of being shot by the archers, the mutant monkeys begin flapping their wings, which now are large enough to support them in flight. They rise high in the air before flying over the walls of Korivan, Once clear of the city, they fly toward the eastern border of Ventryvia.

37.

Kylandar turns to me and asks, "Do you have copies of those magic pictures we've been watching?"

"You mean of the demons?"

"That—and of Jonnasloan."

"Yes, and I can show them to other people if you wish."

"Good. Are you also able to either get a message to N'Shawn or bring him here?"

"Yes. I should be able to do either one. What do you have in mind?"

"I need to prepare an effective counterattack to reclaim my throne. N'Shawn is the logical choice to lead the attack. The first step will probably be to show him what's been happening."

"I can do that, Sire."

I cup my hand over my left ear and say, "Vicky, activate N'Shawn's transceiver."

The initial static is quickly replaced by the quiet words, "This is N'Shawn."

"N'Shawn, this is Max Strider. King Kylandar wants to visit with you."

"King?" he says in a confused voice.

"Yeah, King. That's one of the things you need to know about. Are you available to visit with him privately?"

"When and where?"

"As soon as possible—and we'd prefer bringing you to my place in Hidden Canyon."

"I'm finishing up maneuvers with the Dragon Company. As soon as I get through with that, I should be able to go."

"All right. Contact me when you're ready."

38.

N'Shawn calls a little over an hour later, and I transport him to Hidden Canyon. He watches the videos, is briefed by all of us, and has his questions answered. Together we discuss possible plans for how to attack Jonnasloan's forces.

"I see at least two major problems," N'Shawn says as we finish brainstorming ideas. He nods to Kylandar while continuing, "The people of Ventryvia—including our armed forces—think you have abdicated your throne and installed Jonnasloan as king, which means he starts with an assumption of legitimacy that must be overcome. Plus, even if we are successful in mobilizing opposition, he may be able to command an army of evil demons."

"Possibly," acknowledges Rhylene. "But it seems to me that the more that demons infest the land, the more disenchanted people are likely to become with Jonnasloan. Even if they think Dad voluntarily relinquished the throne, they may want a warrior to be their leader. In other words, they may be ready for him to take control again. More than ready, in fact."

"I understand, and you make a good point," N'Shawn says. "But my men and I have sworn our allegiance to Ventryvia's king. If your father had voluntarily relinquished his throne in favor of Jonnasloan, our loyalties would be pledged to his successor even though our hearts and minds might favor Kylandar. That's why it's important that you present the evidence you showed me." He looks squarely at me and asks, "Can you do that?"

"Yes," I respond. "Let's work out the details of when, where, and how."

39.

Jonnasloan looks across his desk at Premander K'Shay, gestures toward the two caged demons, and says, "I want you to organize a reconnaissance squadron or task force to determine the level of threat these creatures pose to Ventryvia, and formulate a plan for dealing with it. You don't have to lead it, but I want you to pick the leader and give him whatever support he needs. The task force doesn't have to be limited to men under your command. If you need a person from the private sector, get him. If we must negotiate terms, do what you can and then get back with me for final approval. But I need answers quickly."

"Answers quickly—but what are your questions?"

"Where did these things come from? Are there more of them? For that matter, is there anything else coming? Where are they now, and how many are there? Are they likely to continue their attacks?

"Talk to the people who were harmed by these creatures. Find out all you can about the attacks and what happened to the folks they stung or bit. Use your best judgment in setting up and running the task force, but get me intelligence I can rely on, and do it quickly."

"Yes, sire."

"Any questions?"

"Not at this time, sire."

K'Shay salutes, leaves the room, and goes to his office, where he prepares and seals a set of orders. Next he walks to the military barracks, where he commands a courier to take the orders to Premender N'Shawn immediately.

40.

N'Shawn and I are busy mapping out strategy for leading a rebellion against Jonnasloan when Vicky tells us there's something we need to watch, and puts video of K'Shay's meetings with Jonnasloan and with the courier on the screens.

"It appears you are about to be ordered to assemble and lead a task force," I say to him.

"I agree. What will that do to our planned rebellion?"

"It'll probably delay it some, but it will also put us in a position to gather information about the demons before we have to face them."

I give him quavalor gloves, a syringe, and an analyzing rod, and explain how to use each of them.

"You expect me to believe that these little gloves will protect me from a demon's sting?" he asks.

"N'Shawn, these little gloves will even stop bullets."

"They'll stop what?"

"Uh," I stammer while thinking, *They don't have guns here, dummy! He's not going to know anything about bullets!* "Let me demonstrate."

I lead him outside to a bare patch of earth, put the gloves on the ground, and tell him to try to pierce them with his sword. He pokes at one of them.

"No," I tell him. "Hit it hard—as if your life depended upon it."

He responds by giving a glove a mighty blow with his blade. Then he picks up the glove and gasps, "I can't believe it. Not even a nick!"

He puts the gloves back on the ground and attempts to pierce them with the sharp point of the sword. Still nothing.

"Wow! I wish my armor was this good!"

"I may be able to get you some armor made out of the material if that's what you want."

"Absolutely! If you can, that'd be great."

We continue talking while walking around the lake, I give him a fanny pack filled with special equipment and tell him how to use each item, and then Vicky transports him back to Trojhalter.

41.

Later that same day the courier dispatched by K'Shay delivers his message to N'Shawn. After reading the orders, N'Shawn packs the gear he wishes to take with him, shows the orders to his second in command, and places both the Dragon Company and the King's Regiment under his assistant's command during the time he will be gone. Then N'Shawn accompanies the courier back to Van Seissling.

When they arrive at the capitol, they immediately report to Premander K'Shay, who takes N'Shawn to Jonnasloan's office to show him the two caged demons.

"May I take them to a room without windows to examine them more closely?" N'Shawn asks.

"The guest bedroom through that door doesn't have windows," Jonnasloan replies, "but be extremely careful. Those things are dangerous."

"Thank you, sire." N'Shawn picks up the cage and carefully carries it into the adjoining room.

Closing the door, N'Shawn takes the quavalor gloves out of his fanny pack and puts them on. Then he unlocks the cage, carefully opens the cage door, and grasps hold of the wingless demon.

The demon immediately tries to sting N'Shawn, but is unable to pierce the quavalor glove that holds him.

N'Shawn catches sight of the other demon attempting to open the cage door, quickly moves back that direction, and slams the door on the winged demon just as it succeeded in prying the door open. After relocking the cage to bar any further escapes, N'Shawn presses the wingless demon's body against the top of a dresser, withdraws a syringe from the fanny pack, and injects the needle into the demon's stinger. He carefully withdraws venom from the stinger before returning the demon to its cage and locking it.

    N'Shawn takes a small glass jar about the size of a jigger from the fanny pack, squirts in venom from the syringe, and places an analyzing rod into it. He waits about a minute before contacting Vicky, who runs an analysis of the venom.

42.

N'Shawn uses his transceiver to contact me after he leaves the palace. I direct him to go to the tailor shop owned and operated by friends we both know in Van Seissling. N'Shawn had previously worked with the tailors' son, Jamistan, and all of them knew me from when I had lived with them a little over a year ago. Since they have also been transported by me, they are familiar with my "magical" way of traveling.

After giving the tailors a brief explanation, N'Shawn goes into their back workroom, and I transport him from there to Hidden Canyon. We go over his orders together, brainstorm for ideas a bit, and then go into my office.

"Here's what it looked like when the demons were first escaping from Abaddon," I say while showing him video of their mass exodus from Wizard's Island in Lake Zaragon. We watch both sets of demons flying from the island, and again look at their attacks on people in and around Korivan.

"You say the demons escaped from Abaddon," N'Shawn says, "but have you actually seen what's down in that hole?"

"No."

"So we don't really know for certain that it's Abaddon—or if they're coming from some other place that might lead to Abaddon."

I grimace and shrug.

"We also don't know what else is down there—or what might be coming next."

"I'm—uh—I'm afraid not."

"Do you have any way of exploring it, or do I have to go in person?"

"I've got a way to do it." I answer before speaking into my transceiver, "Vicky, how many probes do we have at Wizard's Island?"

"Nine, sir. All are flying probes that can take and transmit pictures even in zero lux darkness."

"Send five of them into the opening into Abaddon. We need to explore what's there."

"Roger that, sir."

43.

Kylandar sticks his head through the doorway of my office and asks, "Did I hear you say you're sending some of those spy thingies into that hole that the flying demons came out of?"

"Yes, you heard correctly, Your Majesty."

"Mind if I sit in on this? I never realized demons could infest our land merely by flying through a hole in the ground. I'd like to see if there isn't more to it than just that."

"You're certainly welcome to stay—and we'd like your input as well."

Vicky has turned on all three of the large monitors mounted on the back wall of my office. They initially show the exterior of the hole through which the demons emerged when they invaded Ventryvia, but then change as they show transmissions from each of the first three probes that are flying into the abyss.

The first probe enters the hole without incident, pausing momentarily to give us a more detailed look at the sides of the entryway. A heavy haze hangs over the entrance, making it difficult to see very far into the gloomy cavern. As the probe flies cautiously into the muck, the cameras adjust to the low light conditions, and Vicky moves its flight path around several obstacles.

The hazy gloom clears after about thirty or forty feet as the probe slowly flies through the cavern and down through a hole to a lower level.

I turn to Kylandar and say, "I don't understand why caverns like this wouldn't be filled with water."

"Why's that?"

"Well, these caves are under an island in a lake. It doesn't make sense to me why the caverns aren't filled with water from the lake—or at least partially filled with rain water."

"And I don't understand why a wizard such as you, Max, should question the existence of magic in our world—especially if you've ever seen the floating islands of Illa Dunne."

"I've never seen those, Your Majesty, though I would like to do so." I turn back to the monitor as the probe approaches a rear wall that appears to be quivering.

I say into my transceiver, "Vicky, move one of the probes near that wall; see if we can determine why it's jerking back and forth at the edges."

The second probe moves within a few feet of the left edge of the wall and hovers there, motionless, while the first probe moves toward the center of the opening and examines it from that angle. The third probe flies toward the right edge of the wall, taking a position there. We study the visual images from all three probes.

The area next to the opening appears to be the normal rock of the cavern—but the edges are constantly in motion, quivering as if attempting to repair the gash in the wall formed by the open hole. Extending across the opening is some type of membrane or force field that looks somewhat like a tightly stretched curtain that is shimmering in the darkness and glowing as if some type of red-hued light is being projected onto it from the other side.

Neither the shimmering membrane nor the quivering edges of rock along the edges of the opening appear natural. I find myself wondering if some battle is going on between unseen forces in conflict.

"What in the world—" I mutter.

"I think the wall's attempting to close up the hole," Kylandar says.

"You may be right," I remark, "but why does it then suddenly reverse itself and get bigger again?"

"Good question," N'Shawn answers. "I don't see anything that appears to be causing it—at least not from this side."

"I don't either," I say while the probes move back and forth along the membrane curtain, showing us various views and angles. "Vicky, move one of the probes through the opening so we can examine it from the other side."

The first probe moves up to the curtain and slowly pushes its way through. As it does, the visual image on the center screen is blanked out by brilliant light, and then the picture is totally lost, being replaced by static.

"What happened?" asks Kylandar.

"Vicky!" I almost shout into my transceiver. "What's going on?"

"I'm not sure. Stand by, please, while I try a few things."

The center screen continues to show nothing but static, but then the static seems to spread to the other two screens as well. After a few minutes, a pixilated image shows up on the center screen, pauses there momentarily, and then snaps into focus. The probe's camera again shows us the membrane curtain, which looks similar to its appearance from the other side, but looks a bit less like a physical object and . . .

"More like a force field," I mutter.

"A forced field?" N'Shawn asks.

"No. A force field."

"What's that?"

"It can be one of several different things—but most commonly is either a vector field acting on particles in space or is a barrier made up of energy, plasma or particles. I used force fields a year ago to protect both King Kylandar and myself in our battles with Wizard Malmortiken."

"Is that what this is?"

"I don't know . . . Probably not, since it doesn't make sense to me why a shield type would be used here—but it still looks somewhat like a vector field."

"I heard your words, but don't know what you said," N'Shawn grumbles.

I don't answer. Instead, I continue to study the left and right screens, which are now completely blank.

"Vicky," I ask. "Why did we lose the video feeds from the other two probes?"

"When the first probe went through the vector curtain, it seems to have entered a different dimension that prevents transmission back to us. I moved the other two probes up to the curtain and put them into portal-to-portal contact with each other before moving one of them through the curtain so that it can receive transmissions from the probe already in that dimension—and then it retransmits its data through the curtain to the probe on this side, which forwards the transmission on to us. It's the only way I can get it to work."

The camera finishes its examination of the membrane curtain and turns toward the area adjacent to it. The rocks and colors on this side of the curtain look different from those on the other side. The hole on Wizard's Island led to a cool dark cavern, but the rocks on this side appear hotter, more volcanic, and colored with a strange fiery red-orange hue.

"What's that?" N'Shawn suddenly exclaims, jumping up from his chair and pointing to a spot on the center screen where the probe shows some creatures in long dark robes standing together at the edge of a column of rock in a small tunnel-like hole or cavern high above a much larger cavern that opens out to one side of them.

"What are they doing?" I ask.

"I'm not sure," N'Shawn answers, "but look at how their attention is directed toward the wavering wall."

"Vicky," I say, "get a probe in close to them—close enough to where we can hopefully hear what they're saying."

We watch the center screen as the picture changes to a view of the creatures as seen from above and slightly to their rear. The sound is enhanced so we can hear what they're saying.

There appear to be four humanoid critters in dark brown hooded robes tightly clustered around a massive black book with strange markings on its pages. Their clothing is similar to the attire worn by medieval monks, and they remind me of the Jawas in some of the old *Star Wars* movies except that they're taller and more grotesque than that pygmy race, and their hands resemble bird claws. Like the fictional Jawas, however, their eyes appear to glow in the dark of their hooded faces—almost like glowing embers.

They're chanting something over and over, but I don't recognize the language. I glance at Kylandar and see that his face appears ashen.

"What's wrong?" I ask.

"I think they're chanting a spell to keep the wall leading to the entrance into Ventryvia open."

After watching them for a while, I have Vicky send the probe on into the cavern while we follow its progress on the center monitor.

As the probe moves into the main cavern, we look out across a vast caldera that is pockmarked with erupting volcanoes, fiery lakes of liquid lava, and active geysers. But unlike the ones in Yellowstone and Iceland that shoot water into the sky, these geysers erupt with molten lava.

Although no moon or stars are visible and inky darkness has replaced the sunlight of the outside world, the rivers and lakes of lava give off enough light that we have no problem seeing details of the landscape as our probe flies over the strange world of burning brimstone and liquid fire.

The volcanic mountains shake with eruptions, expelling clouds of ash and pumice, while glowing lava flows from fissures in the mountains' sides in long red streams like blood, or in orange and yellow streams like molten candy. The various lava streams join together to form glowing rivers that work their way to huge fiery lakes of fire and brimstone.

In the midst of the lakes are islands that appear as black silhouettes against their fiery surroundings.

"Vicky," I say into my transceiver. "Move the probe toward that large island that seems to have creatures moving around on it."

We watch as the video image moves in that direction before stopping and hovering in place.

"Because of the extreme heat, this is about as close as I can safely bring the probe," Vicky announces, "but I'll use the telephoto zoom lens to make the images larger."

Although the picture is somewhat obscured by smoke and steam rising from the burning lakes that surround the island and by ash from the numerous volcanoes, we are able to observe hundreds of humanoid creatures gathered in ranks and files. Most of them are dressed similarly to the ones we saw earlier chanting their spell near the membrane curtain, though some of them appear to be wearing armor or something else that's bulky or padded. All of them have some type of sticks that resemble guns.

"What in the world?" I mutter.

N'Shawn explains, "They appear to be several companies of warriors carrying blow tubes as their weapons."

"Blow *tubes*?" I ask.

"Yes. They are used to blow small projectiles—such as poisoned darts—at a target."

Of course, I think. *They call them blow tubes here rather than blowguns because they aren't familiar with guns. Makes sense.*

As the probe hovers motionless over the island, I become aware of shadows flying around us in all directions. At first I can't make out what type of flying creature they are, but then I spot one hovering on an air thermal rising from the lake, am able to study it, and determine that it's a flying reptile similar to a pterodactyl. These creatures seem to be patrolling the area.

"Try to keep our probe away from those flying things," I tell Vicky.

The probe moves on, keeping its distance from the flying shadows as much as possible. Numerous additional islands appear, almost all of them populated with warriors clad similarly to the ones I first observed. There are a few exceptions. Some islands contain creatures that are not clothed in either robes or armor, which gives me a chance to study their bodies. They stand on two legs like humans, but their legs and backs are deformed, their structure appearing similar to birds, with hands resembling claws.

Floating around and above the islands are gossamer apparitions that appear more like spirits than physical beings. These spirits seem to rise out of the lakes of fire and float through the air without effort or use of wings. They are smaller than the warriors and possess bodies that are vaguely human in form that glimmer like pale green fireflies, though with a translucent luminance that partially offsets their transparency.

After studying those creatures for a few minutes, I tell Vicky to let the probe continue exploring the cavern. Although the scene keeps changing with new volcanoes, geysers, and lakes of fire everywhere, the similarity of it all makes it seem as if this fiery world will continue forever.

I do, however, notice at least one subtle change: The islands of warriors thin out and eventually disappear, and the inhabitants that replace them seem less substantial, less solid, and more ethereal. They also look more human, though lacking solid structure. They remind me of the way Hollywood depicts human ghosts.

The islands have also been getting smaller and more isolated even though the number of creatures has remained about the same. Thus, more and more of these poor unfortunate souls or humanoid ghosts (as I've come to think of them) are actually walking or swimming in the vast lake of fire. Indeed, some of them seem to even be playing there! But how could that be? How could anyone frolic in the flames?

I'm incredulous at the sight. Fire surrounds them, and the probe registers high levels of gas from burning sulfur and brimstone. In addition to the intense heat, it must really smell horrible! How can they stand being there? But then again, what choice do they have?

Sprinkled among the captive souls are other beings who are less human and more grotesque. They stand upright on their hind legs like people, but their arms and hands are misshaped and grotesque in appearance. They carry whips, swords and pitchforks, which they use to inflict additional pain and torment upon the unfortunate prisoners assigned to them.

As I scan the vista before me, I realize that I don't see any cavern walls. Instead, the lakes of fire continue for as far as I can see—or at least until it is obscured by rising smoke and steam.

I turn to Kylandar. "This place is immense! Is all of this really under Lake Zaragon and the surrounding area?"

"I think not," he answers. "I strongly suspect that shimmering curtain we passed through probably separates the cavern under Wizard's Island and Lake

Zaragon from this place, which is somewhere else altogether."

"What *is* this place?"

"I'm pretty sure it's Abaddon."

"Oh!" I mumble. And then I think it through.

It stands to reason that Abaddon would be in a different dimension from the cavern under Wizard's Island. After all, Abaddon is another name for Hell, a place prepared for Satan and his demons. In other words, it may be in a spiritual dimension rather than a physical one. The shimmering curtain may be some type of portal that connects the two.

Nevertheless, Abaddon is physical enough that our probe can visit and transmit pictures back to us. Although I don't understand it, I know the prudent course of action is to use this opportunity to learn all I can about Abaddon and the enemies we're likely to face from there.

As I look over the grotesque panorama spread out before me and consider its strange inhabitants, I suddenly realize something's missing. "Wait!" I cry. "Where are the flying scorpions?"

"The what?" asks N'Shawn.

"Flying scorpions. Ventryvia was invaded by several swarms of flying insect-like creatures that stung people. I haven't seen any of those things here. Have you seen any?"

"You're right," says Kylandar. "I haven't seen any either."

"Maybe the ones that have already appeared are all that there are," N'Shawn adds.

"Maybe," I concede, "but I have my doubts. Vicky, see what you can find."

A few minutes later Vicky reports, "Sir, here's what I've found," and puts an image on the screen of thousands of the creatures resting on rocks high above the lakes of fire. Above them are additional multitudes of bat-like creatures hanging from the ceiling of the cavern.

"I guess we didn't see them earlier because they weren't flying around drawing attention to themselves," I say.

"And because they are so much smaller than the other creatures, we didn't see them in the darkness," Kylandar adds.

"Yeah, but I think I see something else," Rhylene says as she moves closer to the video screen. "What's *that* thing?" she asks while pointing at a dark object on an island just barely visible in the distance.

"Vicky," I order, "move the probe closer to the object Rhylene is pointing at."

As the probe moves through the mists toward the island, it becomes clearer that what Rhylene saw is a massive fortress that appears to balance towers atop battlements with interlinking parapets, flying buttresses, and intertwined catwalks that defy description. The castle portion of the fortress rises so high its upper portions aren't discernable through the mists. Surrounding the structure on all sides are squadrons of flying demons patrolling the area.

"Don't get too close," I warn. "We don't want them to spot our probe."

The probe backs away, and then flies around the fortress, studying it from a safer distance. It then turns and looks out away from the fortress. The lakes of fire extend in all directions with innumerable islands rising through the flames and smoke. Armies of demons and other captive souls populate the cavern in quantities beyond number.

"This place is immense!" I again mutter to myself. All the armies of Ventryvia would only be a drop in the bucket compared to the legions of demons opposing them.

"Oh Lord! What chance do we have? How can we stand against them?" I wonder aloud.

Rhylene, Kylandar and N'Shawn glance at me. The fear and dread I feel is reflected in their eyes as well.

44.

I'm sitting at my desk watching the video screens with Kylandar and Rhylene. After several days of studying Abaddon and its inhabitants, N'Shawn has gone back to Van Seissling to report to Jonnasloan, and we are interested in seeing what happens. N'Shawn and Kylandar have also been able to discuss various objectives, tactics and battle plans that could be used in their battle against Jonnasloan for control of Ventryvia.

We watch as N'Shawn and K'Shay are admitted to Jonnasloan's office. After saluting, N'Shawn unrolls a map of Ventryvia and briefs the other men about the demons of Abaddon and the netherworld from which they seem to have come. The two military men discuss options and strategy, concluding that the best place for resisting the armies of demons would be at the place they enter Ventryvia.

After N'Shawn answers the others' questions, he is dismissed and allowed to return to his post in Trojhalter. Jonnasloan and K'Shay continue their deliberations.

"I don't like the idea of demons invading our land," Jonnasloan says. "However, since the demons that stung people around Korivan didn't attack our armed forces, I'm hesitant to attack them, since that might provoke a full-scale invasion."

K'Shay responds, "I understand, but it would be naïve not to prepare for such an invasion."

"What do you propose?"

"I think I should go there and see for myself what Premander N'Shawn observed. I could take some of my top assistants with me to help formulate battle strategy."

"Very well, K'Shay. Do it—and then report back to me."

45.

Three days later Premander K'Shay pauses as he crests a hill with a small company of men. Below them lies Lake Zaragon. K'Shay turns and looks at the men accompanying him. He considered bringing the Dragon Company, since its soldiers were reputed to be the best fighters in the army. But that company had been led by N'Shawn for years and was loyal to him.

At one time the two men were close friends. Indeed, K'Shay still liked N'Shawn and fully respected him even though they had fought on opposite sides during Wizard Malmortiken's rebellion against King Kylandar. It wasn't that K'Shay had anything against Kylandar; it was just that he feared Malmortiken and what the Wizard might do to him and his family if he opposed him.

N'Shawn followed K'Shay's commands and did what he was told. In other words, he's a good soldier. But they no longer were as close as they had been before the rebellion. Besides, N'Shawn and his Dragon Company were stationed in Trojhalter, which was out of the way when going from Van Seissling to Lake Zaragon. At least that was K'Shay's rationalization for not bringing them along as part of this group.

On the other hand, these men are soldiers I fully trust; they're totally loyal to me.

K'Shay turns in his saddle and signals for his aide d'camp, Requinder M'Kiver, to join him on the ridge overlooking Lake Zaragon.

"It's too late in the day to explore Wizard's Island now. Have the men set up camp along the shore, set watches and security for the night, and then join me and Requinder L'Raisson in my tent."

As the men later gather around a map in K'Shay's tent, he points out that "this map is not totally up to date, since it still identifies the Wizard's Tower as being on the small island in front of us—when in fact the tower was destroyed in the final battle with Wizard Malmortiken."

He looks at the other men, smiles, and continues, "I bring this up because Wizard's Island is where we believe the demons that attacked some of our citizens in Korivan came from—and that's where we will begin our reconnaissance."

"What makes you think that's where they came from?" L'Raisson asks.

"Because that's what Premander N'Shawn said when he delivered his report to King Jonnasloan and me last week. I had sent him on an exploratory mission to determine where the demons originated, where they had gone, and anything else he could discover about them.

"He says there's a cavern under Wizard's Island that seems to lead to an underworld where the demons live. Quite frankly, I didn't fully understand what he said—which is one of the primary reasons I want to see it for myself. I brought you along to help me map out our strategy for dealing with them. I trust you men and know from past experience that we can work well together."

Turning to L'Raisson, K'Shay says, "Tomorrow morning I want you to send a few soldiers into the cavern to explore the area. I want us to accompany them as observers. In other words, they'll probe while we observe, take notes, and formulate strategy."

46.

Wizard's Island owes its name to the fact that it had been the location of Wizard Malmortiken's tower, which was his residence when he chose to be away from the palace in Van Seissling. However, the tower had been destroyed during his battle with King Kylandar and Max Strider, and Malmortiken had perished shortly afterward.

The soldiers accompanying Premander K'Shay are up before dawn the next morning, have breakfast, and advance to Wizard's Island. They climb the hill where the tower had stood before descending into the hole remaining under the spot where the tower had been. Along the western edge of the hole is the entrance to the caverns K'Shay plans to explore.

Four squads of soldiers cautiously enter the cavern. A squad of archers accompany armored knights as the recon group, while a similar assortment provide security for the military commanders who are observing and taking notes. The rest of the company has taken positions on Wizard's Island outside the cavern and are responsible for providing security as well as being a reserve force.

Magic floating balls of light provide illumination for the soldiers as they move forward through the cavern, which slopes downward for about thirty yards before dropping away. Ropes are brought forward and used to lower three soldiers into the hole, where they look around with the aid of the balls of light. They report that the cavern continues northward and appears to be relatively level.

A fifth squad of soldiers is brought into the cavern to stay with the ropes, and the first four squads plus the military commanders lower themselves down to the lower level of the cavern. After reassembling on the lower level, the soldiers move forward through the cave, follow it as it doglegs to the right, and then stop abruptly at a rear wall that at first appears to be glowing with a translucent orange-hued light.

Most of the rear wall is composed of rock like the other parts of the cavern. But the center portion of it resembles a curtain or screen made up of small particles floating in the air. The soldiers gape at it in amazement and then look at each other as if asking what they should do.

After a few moments one of the soldiers—perhaps braver or more fool-hardy than the others—creeps toward the curtain and reaches out to touch it. He pokes at it with a finger. When nothing adverse happens, he puts his hand through the particle curtain before pulling back and examining himself. Next he pokes his entire right arm through, holds it there momentarily, and then follows his arm with his head—and suddenly disappears.

The other soldiers wait expectantly for him to reappear, but seconds turn into minutes and nothing happens. Finally, another soldier crouches next to the particle curtain, talking to himself in an apparent effort to build up his confidence. After a few moments he puts first his hand and then his entire arm through before pulling back and talking with the soldier nearest to him.

Both men crawl back up to the curtain. The first man lies prone while inching forward. As he pokes his head through the streaming particles, his body shudders, jerks twice, and then lies still. The second soldier grabs the other's legs, pulls him back to this side of the curtain, and calls for assistance.

"What's wrong?" yells K'Shay.'

"He's unconscious and his face is burning hot!"

"Get the healer."

The healer hustles up to the man, examines him, and says, "He seems to be suffering from heat stroke."

"Heat stroke—in a cave away from the sun?" another soldier asks.

"I know," admits the healer. "It doesn't make sense to me either, but that's what his symptoms indicate."

Two other soldiers carry their fallen comrade back out of the way where he can be treated by the healer, and K'Shay visits with his top advisors away from the other soldiers.

"Didn't you tell us Premander N'Shawn has already explored this cavern?" asks L'Raisson.

"That's right. He reported his findings to King Jonnasloan and me."

"What did he report about this area?"

"I don't remember anything particularly out of the ordinary. He mentioned this strange particle curtain, but didn't say anything about the problems we're encountering here. He said there were several strange creatures on the other side of it that were chanting something in a language he didn't recognize."

"But he said nothing about having trouble getting past the curtain?"

"Nothing that I recall. He must have got through here all right because he fully described the creatures, islands and volcanoes he saw."

"Volcanoes?"

"That's right. Volcanoes spewing ash, smoke and lava—all of which flowed down into lakes of fire."

"And all of that was right on the other side of that curtain?"

"That's what he said, though he also claimed the sides of the curtain were vibrating and snapping back and forth as if the walls were trying to close up the opening in the rock wall."

The men look back at the wall with the particle curtain and study it for a few moments.

"Well," Requinder M'Kiver mutters, "It is vibrating some, but that's about it— No, wait. It seems to be changing."

"Yes, you're right," agrees L'Raisson. "The hole in the wall is getting bigger and seems to be changing color, becoming a deeper orange."

"And what are those things?" asks M'Kiver, pointing toward faint wispy creatures that suddenly appear to be flying through the curtain.

Hundreds of ghost-like almost transparent creatures stream through the opening. Some of them fly to the soldiers near the curtain and appear to be absorbed into the men's bodies, but most of them stream on through the cavern and up through the hole to the upper level.

The soldiers whose bodies were invaded immediately begin arguing and fighting with one another, cursing and calling each other despicable names, and slashing each other with their swords and other weapons.

Within moments all the soldiers in the two squads that had been in front of the curtain lie dead. As the men die, the semi-transparent spirits that invaded their bodies exit and continue out of the cavern.

The only men remaining alive are the three commanding officers and the two squads who had served as their security guard. They stand speechless, their eyes wide in shock at the horror they've just witnessed, though one soldier is bent over, vomiting and convulsing.

"If we hadn't been way over here and totally out of the way, we would also have been attacked," M'Kiver mutters.

"Almost certainly," agrees K'Shay, "but what were those things?"

"Some kind of demons or evil spirits," says L'Raisson. "Whatever they are, they're deadly."

"Agreed. We need to get out of here. Follow me back to the ropes—but quietly. And stay next to the wall in the shadows."

The surviving soldiers move cautiously through the cavern until they reach the hole leading to the upper level—but are able to go no further, since the ropes are still above the opening.

"This is Premander K'Shay," he yells. "Drop the ropes for us."

No response.

He calls twice more but gets no answer. "Is there another way out?" he asks.

His companions look at one another and shrug that they don't know. K'Shay divides his guards into three-man teams and sends them in different directions to explore the cavern.

47.

"Sir! Check your center monitor!" Vicky exclaims.

Kylandar and I immediately turn and stare at the images streaming across the middle screen in my office. A multitude of gossamer creatures floats around one of the towers of the massive fortress one of our probes has been watching.

"Vicky, see if you can get a closer image of what those creatures are doing around that tower."

As the lens zooms in, I can see there's an indistinct figure standing on a balcony high up on the tower apparently giving instructions to the ghostly apparitions floating around it. Because the thing—whatever it is—is standing in the deep shadows of the balcony and is surrounded by semi-transparent beings, I can't get a good look at it, but when it disappears back into the tower, the multitude of ghosts moves away from the fortress and flies toward the portal leading to our world.

"What's happening?" Rhylene asks as she pokes her head through the doorway.

"We don't know yet," her father replies. "Come in and watch with us."

The gossamer cloud pauses as it approaches the portal, and additional chanters join the ones we initially observed. Together, they direct their attention toward the portal, which enlarges and changes color, becoming a brighter orange than before.

The creatures begin flying into the curtain of suspended particles, disappearing from the picture on our center screen as they do. Seconds after the first one disappears, it reappears on our right screen, which shows the rear wall of the cavern under Wizard's Island—and the ghosts flying through the curtain as viewed from that side.

We watch as the apparition flies out of the curtain, collides with a soldier, and seems to be absorbed into the man's body. He immediately turns and yells insults at the other soldiers near him. But they've also been invaded by ghost-like creatures, and they respond by attacking one another. Within minutes all the men near the particle curtain are dead. As they die, the semi-transparent creatures leave and fly on toward the entrance to the cave.

We sit in stunned silence for a minute or two before I mutter, "What happened? What did we just see?"

"A massacre," Kylandar responds grimly.

"I'm going to be sick," Rhylene gasps.

"I feel the same," Kylandar says. "We're fortunate there weren't more men there—or there would have been even more casualties."

"But there are more," Rhylene says, pointing at the screen. "Look back over there in the shadows."

She's right. The three commanding officers and their guards appear to still be unharmed. We watch as they visit among themselves briefly before making their way to the hole leading to the upper level. They yell for the ropes to be dropped but get no answer.

"Vicky! Show us what's happened to the ropes."

"Just a moment, sir. I'll get a probe over there."

As the probe swings around the cavern into position, we see the ropes lying on the floor of the upper level near the hole to the lower level—and lying on top of the ropes are bodies of the dead soldiers assigned to guard them.

48.

"They've been wiped out, too!" Kylandar mutters.

"Vicky, show us what's happened to the soldiers outside the caverns," I order.

"Yes, sir," Vicky responds while turning on the left monitor in my office.

Dead bodies litter the cavern entrance. The probe's camera slowly pans the landscape, showing more lifeless soldiers.

One of the men stirs, sits up, and then stands. He shakes himself and looks around at his dead comrades. A sudden movement catches his eye as he sees an archer about eighty yards away, walking toward him. He bellows a threatening challenge at the archer, draws his sword and charges, waving his sword as he runs.

The startled archer raises his bow defensively and yells, "Carson! It's me, Franklin!"

The swordsman continues his charge, bellowing crazily.

"Carson, what are you doing? Stop! Don't come any closer! I don't want to shoot—but I will."

As the swordsman rushes to within about twenty yards, the archer draws back on his bow and fires an arrow into the first man's chest. The swordsman staggers and falls, but then picks himself up and charges again. The archer puts two more arrows through his attacker before the crazed soldier collapses and dies. As his life expires, we see a gossamer apparition rise from the corpse and float away.

Franklin backs away, still holding an arrow in firing position while exclaiming, "Sorry, old buddy, but you left me no choice."

The probe's camera pulls back from the scene, showing dead bodies littering the landscape. Only the lone archer appears to still be alive—but he seems reluctant to approach his fallen comrades that lie between him and the caverns. Instead, he moves back and hides behind some boulders.

"Vicky, is there any other way for the soldiers on the lower level of the cavern to get to the upper level except through the hole with the ropes?"

"Not that I know of, sir—other than magic."

"Magic? What do you mean?"

"Well, Wizard Malmortiken could levitate himself."

"Yeah, but he was a powerful wizard. Have you seen anything other than the ropes that could help K'Shay and his men?"

"No, sir."

"Then I've got to help them," I say as I get to my feet. "I'm going to the meadow so you can transport me. Be ready to send me to a safe spot near the ropes."

49.

After reaching the meadow beyond the waterfall, I say, "All right, Vicky. I'm ready."

I feel a sudden tugging at my midsection, coupled with the familiar darkness and cold of the void as the red walls of Hidden Canyon are replaced with the dark interior of the caverns under Wizard' Island.

As my eyes adjust to the semi-darkness, I see two floating balls of light positioned near the hole leading down to the lower level. I crouch down and whisper into my transceiver, "Vicky, warn me if any more of those spirit creatures fly through the portal."

"Will do, sir."

I look around at the cavern floor illuminated by the balls of light. About ten feet from me are the ropes needed by the men down below. I make certain the ropes are securely anchored to rock columns, move a dead body that is covering the free ends, and then push the ropes over the edge, allowing them to fall through the hole.

"Sir!" I hear shouted from below. "These ropes have just been dropped down to us."

"Are they secure?"

"This one appears to be. . . Yes, sir. Both ropes are securely fastened to something."

"Hello, up there," the commander's voice yells to me. "Show yourself. I have a few questions I need answered."

Should I respond? K'Shay doesn't know me and would undoubtedly want to know how I knew he and his troops were in trouble—which lets him know I'm observing his mission. The principal time we met was while he was helping Wizard Malmortiken fight against King Kylandar. We were on opposite sides then—and might be now as well, since he serves Jonnasloan instead of Kylandar.

I briefly consider remaining here and visiting with K'Shay but decide it will probably be better to leave. *He might have too many questions I'd have a hard time answering without disclosing information I'd rather not discuss with him.*

"Vicky!" I whisper into my transceiver. "Transport me out of here."

50.

"What's happening?" I ask as I walk through the doorway to my office.

"So far two soldiers have used the ropes you dropped to climb up to the higher level," Kylandar says. "A third soldier is being pulled up now."

I glance at the monitor in time to see the third soldier climb out of the hole and join his comrades. As those three begin helping a fourth warrior, I ask, "Vicky, have you assigned any probes to watch where the gossamer demons have gone?"

"Yes, sir. Two probes are following them as they fly eastward."

"Do you know where they're going yet?"

"No sir, but I suspect they might be joining the scorpion demons and flying monkeys."

"And where are they?"

"I don't know the name of the place, but I can show you a picture of them on your right monitor, since I've assigned some probes to watch them."

The image on the right screen changes to show dozens of winged monkeys huddled under some trees in a desolate area. At first I don't see any scorpion-cicada demons—but then I realize hundreds of them have infested the trees around the monkeys.

I turn to Kylandar and ask, "Do you recognize the place shown on the right screen?"

"No. It doesn't look at all familiar to me. Why do you ask?"

"Because that's where the demons have gone."

"Can you show me on a map?"

"No, Your Majesty; I don't have a map here. Wait a minute! I might be able to, after all." I mumble into my transceiver, "Vicky, can you overlay the demons' position onto a high overhead picture of the area? You know, showing the rivers and seacoast and other major identifiable features?"

"I think so—but it will take me a few minutes."

"Do it. Let us know when you're ready to show it to us."

"Yes, sir."

We turn back to the other screens and watch as the remaining soldiers extricate themselves from the lower level. When K'Shay gets up there, he immediately checks the bodies of each soldier lying on the cavern floor and asks the other officers to check them.

"Quite frankly, I'm puzzled by what I see," K'Shay says. "Someone obviously dropped the ropes down to us—but I don't think it was any of these men, since they have been dead long enough to begin getting stiff around their eyelids, jaws and necks. Yet I don't see anyone or anything else that could have done it. What do you think?"

The other two officers just shrug their shoulders and shake their heads.

K'Shay looks at them expectantly before turning on his heel and muttering, "Well, maybe the answers are around the entrance to the caverns." He begins walking toward the front of the cave.

But instead of answers, all K'Shay finds is more dead bodies littering the landscape. He and his men check each corpse, but find none that could have dropped the ropes that saved them—until a reclusive archer rises from behind a boulder, cautiously steps forward and yells, "Are you safe to approach--or are you crazy like those other guys?"

"We're normal," K'Shay replies. "Step forward and tell us your name and what happened out here."

"I'm Sarheit Franklin," the archer says while walking slowly toward the survivors who had emerged from the caverns. "I'm really not sure what happened, but the entire group of soldiers suddenly went crazy. They started attacking one another—both verbally and with their weapons."

"Why weren't you affected?"

"I don't know, sir—unless it's because I wasn't with the others. I was providing security over by the boulders. When the others went crazy, I slipped behind the rocks and watched and listened."

"Did you get involved in any way?"

"Well, uh . . . I guess I did. Some, anyway."

"How?"

"I got attacked by a man I thought was a friend and—uh . . . And I ended up killing him. He's the one lying right over there," Franklin says while pointing to the prostrate soldier. "I yelled for him to stop, but he kept charging at me, swinging his sword. I'm sorry, sir, but I didn't know of anything else to do."

"I understand, Sarheit. Did you notice anything unusual about him when he died?"

"Now that you mention it—yes, sir. I think I did."

What was it?"

"When he collapsed and stopped breathing, I thought I saw something rise out of his body and fly away. And I think I saw similar things coming out of the other men when they died."

K'Shay exchanges glances with the other officers and they nod to one another.

*****

"Sir," Vicky says through speakers in my office. "I've got what you asked for."

"What's that?"

"You asked me to overlay the demons' position onto a satellite view or map-like picture showing major identifiable features so you could see where the demons are right now. I've done it."

"Show us what you have."

A visual representation of the eastern portion of Ventryvia appears on the left monitor. Wizard's Island is near the top left corner, while Lake Zaragon extends along the top border of the screen with the Andora River flowing out from it and extending to the southern edge.

Van Seissling occupies the lower left corner of the picture near the confluence of the Andora and Reinijara Rivers. The Reinijara extends eastward to the edge of the screen. About halfway between that point and Lake Zaragon is a pulsing curser that represents where the demons have gone. Vicky informs us that the gossamer demons are flying east southeast of Lake Zaragon and appear to be likely to join the other demons.

Kylandar rises from his chair, walks to the left monitor, points to a spot at the bottom of the screen and says, "Ventryvia's eastern border runs due north from here."

"In other words," I clarify, "The demons are just barely past the eastern border."

"That's correct," he affirms. "The first waves of demons are now in a wilderness area right outside our country. Although they are no longer in Ventryvia, they can return very easily and quickly."

51.

Two days later Kylandar and Rhylene join me in my office to watch K'Shay's report to Jonnasloan. When he finishes, the putative king asks a few questions before dismissing K'Shay.

Jonnasloan walks to a large wall map of Ventryvia and studies it before sitting back down at his desk. He opens a drawer, takes out an enchanted mirror, and holds it in front of him, studying its features. Several times he starts to use the mirror, but each time he reconsiders and breaks off the message before really beginning.

He leans forward on the desk, his head between his hands. Then he leans back in his chair, lost deep in thought. Finally he reaches resolutely for the mirror, takes several deep breaths and commands, "Scrymarron Count DeVil."

Several minutes pass before a warped voice replies from the mirror, "This is Count DeVil. Are you trying to contact me?"

"Yes, but I can hardly see or hear you."

"I'll have to boost the power from this end." Silence for a moment. Then the voice changes from being warped to becoming silky smooth. "There. Is that better?"

"Much better."

"What can I do for you?" asks DeVil.

"You can remove your demons. A new batch of them wiped out a company of my soldiers."

"Those soldiers were snooping around the portal to my domain. You need to keep your people away from there."

"This isn't working out the way I'd hoped. I wanted to be king to solve problems facing Ventryvia—but because of the demons, the problems have only grown and become worse. I'm afraid I have no choice but to rescind our agreement that permits your creatures to pass through Ventryvia on their way to other lands."

"All right. I'll agree to renegotiate—but we must do it in person. When can you meet with me?"

"I can see you whenever you get here. Don't allow any more of your *'things'* to enter Ventryvia until then."

"I'll see you shortly."

Jonnasloan turns off the mirror, puts it back into the drawer, and falls back in his chair with a great sigh of relief.

*****

"What do you make of that?" I ask.

"Personally, I don't trust that Count fella any further than I could throw the palace," Kylandar answers.

"I definitely wouldn't want to meet with him privately," adds Rhylene. "I'm not sure I'd be willing to talk with him even if we were surrounded by my best and most loyal troops."

"At least K'Shay's report was rather accurate," Kylandar says. "I bet he still can't figure out how the ropes got dropped to him, though."

"Yeah, I kinda wanted to talk with him, but decided it might be better to skedaddle."

"Skee-what?"

"Uh . . . to leave hastily."

"Sir," Vicky says, "I've recorded something happening in Abaddon you may wish to see."

"What is it?"

"It appears to be Count DeVil, and he's flying from the fortress toward the portal leading to Ventryvia. I'm putting it on your left monitor."

We turn to look at it—and I'm shocked to see a man who looks like Count DeVil *riding on the back of an enormous black winged wolf.*

"I thought that thing was burned to a crisp!" I mutter.

"It was," Kylandar responds. "I saw it happen."

"Then this must be its twin. Both flying wolves are as big as horses."

"Big as what?"

"Sorry. I ran my thoughts together. I meant to say both are as big as a huge sorrak. How many of those creatures are there?"

"I don't know. I'd never seen one prior to the one Malmortiken rode in his battle with you. But it obviously wasn't the *only* one."

"Unless it got resurrected. But if that happened, could Malmortiken also still be alive?"

"Let's not even go there," Kylandar snaps. "No, both man and beast died last year. This is a different flying wolf—but at least we now know where they come from."

"Abaddon?"

"Where else? And this also verifies that DeVil is associated with Abaddon."

"Humph!" snorts Rhylene. "It appears to me he's more than just associated with it."

"I'm afraid you're right," concedes her father as we watch man and wolf fly into the portal shown on our left monitor.

Vicky turns on our right screen so we can watch them emerge from the portal into Ventryvia moments later.

Wolf and rider fly through the caverns to its entrance, and quickly climb into the sky. Soon they are high enough to escape notice from folks on the ground. Even if someone spotted them, they would probably be mistaken for a passing dragon.

"Sir," Vicky says, "We may have a problem."

"What is it?"

"The probe I've assigned to follow DeVil's wolf is flying at its maximum speed—but that's not fast enough to keep up with them."

"Don't we have extra probes in and around Ventryvia's major cities?"

"Yes, sir."

"See what direction they are going and assign some extra flying probes to intercept them."

"Will do, sir."

Two probes from Korivan pick up our quarry at different points as they fly southward near the Andora River, and then three more probes that had been assigned to Van Seissling take over the task. By the time that last probe joins the hunt, I have a pretty good idea where they are heading.

I clear my throat and say to my companions, "DeVil passed Van Seissling without attempting to stop at the palace. I strongly suspect he's going to the country mansion where the three of us were imprisoned."

"Why?" asks Kylandar.

"Isn't it obvious," answers Rhylene. "He wants to pick up something or somebody that's there."

"Or both," I say. "Vicky, do you still have probes in and around that house we're talking about?"

"Yes, sir. I have two flying probes watching it from outside—plus the six small probes you carried inside before they captured you."

"If you can, move the small interior probes to a place where we can try to listen in on DeVil's conversation when he gets there—assuming, of course, that's where he's going."

"Yes, sir."

52.

The country mansion where we were imprisoned does indeed turn out to be Count DeVil's destination. When he arrives, the wolf circles the house once before settling down in the front yard.

DeVil hops off the beast, tells it to wait for him, and trots toward the front door. It opens at his command, and he enters.

"How much of the transformation potion do you have prepared?" DeVil yells to Tybatha as he races through the house.

"About two-thirds of a caldron," she replies.

"Fill three or four flasks with it."

"Now?"

"Yes, as quickly as you can." Turning to Bynum, the Count orders, "Grab your travelling bag and come with me."

Bynum turns and races up the stairs. Moments later he returns with a small black bag. Tybatha enters the room carrying four hip flasks and hands them to DeVil, who passes them on to Bynum, commanding, "Put these into your bag."

As Bynum does so, DeVil adds, "Now come with me."

At the door, DeVil turns and tells Tybatha, "Pack what you need for an extended stay and head to the palace in Van Seissling within the next week or two. And bring whatever potion you can conveniently carry."

She nods and says, "Understood."

The two men walk out the door and climb onto the winged wolf.

53.

The wolf settles down near the edge of a forest to the west of Van Seissling. Its two riders climb off and hike eastward toward the city.

Since both men had been to the palace on various occasions previously with Jonnasloan, soldiers willingly escort them to Jonnasloan's office on the third floor, and then wait with them while Fitzroy announces their presence to the putative king.

Fitzroy returns a few moments later, holds the door open, and beckons, "Come on in."

As Count DeVil and Bynum settle into two chairs facing Jonnasloan's desk, DeVil leans forward and asks pleasantly, "Now, what seems to be the problem that has upset you?"

"The problem," replies Jonnasloan, "is that our agreement has not worked out, and it must be rescinded. I wanted to be king because I honestly believed I could help to make the country better by solving some of its problems. But I haven't been able to even work on those issues because of all the additional problems caused by your demons."

The Count nods smoothly and says, "Yes, I think I understand—and I agree that our covenant has not worked out as well as either of us hoped." He smiles, rises as if to shake Jonnasloan's hand while continuing, "And I agree that it should now be rescinded."

DeVil's right hand stops before reaching Jonnasloan, and he says while smiling, "Parschcoma!"

Jonnasloan's right hand freezes while reaching to shake the Count's hand. He remains rigid momentarily, but then slumps over his desk, his unconscious body gradually falling to the floor.

Turning to Bynum, DeVil orders, "Give me your bag."

Bynum reaches beside his chair, retrieves the bag, and hands it to the Count.

Opening the bag, DeVil removes a small pouch from an inside pocket, takes out a syringe, and uses it to draw blood from his unconscious victim. He then adds the blood to the transformation potion in one of the hip flasks Bynum had brought, shakes the flask thoroughly, and hands it to Bynum.

"Drink!" he commands.

Bynum nods and does as ordered. His transformation into the image of King Jonnasloan—complete with his voice—begins almost immediately. The two men strip Jonnasloan's clothes from his body, and Bynum changes into them.

DeVil levitates Jonnasloan's body, moves it into the guest room, and drops it onto a bed. Turning to Bynum, he says, "I should have made you king in the first place—

but I really thought he would turn out to be more useful and pliable than he was."

"Are you just going to leave him there?" asks Bynum.

"Why not?"

"If he's not restrained, can't he escape?"

"Not while he's under that spell. This way it's easier for you to draw more blood to make additional potion whenever you need it."

"What if I need to revive him?"

"Why would you want to do that?"

"I may need to ask him questions."

"Oh. All right. To put him into a semiconscious coma so he can answer questions but not cause problems, simply put your hand on top of his head and say 'Resplondo!' To put him back into a silent coma, point at him and say 'Parshcoma!'"

"Can you write those down for me?"

DeVil shakes his head disapprovingly but nevertheless walks to the king's desk and writes down the words.

54.

"Well," I say while standing and shaking my head. "Looks like we have a new sheriff in town."

"Sheer if?" Rhylene asks. "What's that mean?"

"It means DeVil has appointed a new leader for Ventryvia."

"Bynum's no leader," says Kylandar. "He's a follower. No, scratch that. He's Count DeVil's lap dog. He's following orders given him by the commander of demons. We've got to take him out before things get worse."

"They're already worse, Your Majesty."

"I'm afraid you're right—but I can't stand idly by watching the country I love become a cesspool of demons."

"I agree, Sire. What are your orders?"

"Orders?"

"Yes, Sire. What do you want us to do? What's your plan?"

"Right now I have no army and no followers other than the two of you. I'd say a good place to start would be to try to increase our numbers."

"How?"

"Get N'Shawn. Bring him here and show him what's happened. Tap his brain; get his ideas and suggestions. I sincerely believe he may be the key to reaching the other military leaders and bringing them into our camp."

"Can the physical strength of the military defeat demons?" I ask.

"I honestly don't know—but we've got to start somewhere."

55.

After contacting N'Shawn on his transceiver, we transport him to Hidden Canyon, where he views the videos Vicky has made and peppers us with questions.

N'Shawn looks Kylandar in the eye and says, "I agree with you that we must have the military on our side in order to stand a chance, but I'm not sure how to accomplish that."

"K'Shay is commander of the army. You need to visit with him and convince him of the danger to Ventryvia if he doesn't lead the troops against Bynum, DeVil and the demons."

"Sorry, Your Majesty, but that won't work."

"Why not?"

"He'll think Bynum is actually Jonnasloan. He's got to see for himself that Bynum's an imposter. Would it be possible for me to bring him here so that he can see the same things I have seen?"

"Yes," I respond. "It's possible—but I don't think it's advisable. Until we know for certain where his loyalties lie, I would rather for him not to know about Hidden Canyon or about our ability to transport or to see what's happening in other places across Ventryvia."

K'Shawn is silent for a moment before saying, "I can understand your rationale—but how can we show him the truth?"

Rhylene answers, "Why not take him there and let him see for himself?"

"What do you mean?" I ask.

"Send N'Shawn to Van Seissling, let him visit with K'Shay, and then—when it's safe to do so—beam both of them into the room where they're keeping Jonnasloan. You might even be able to rescue Jonnasloan as part of the deal."

I look questioningly at N'Shawn. He shrugs and says, "Yeah, that just might work."

I shake my head and grimace, "But that still reveals both our ability to transport and the fact that we can see things that are happening even in the privacy of the king's chambers."

Kylandar responds, "I agree it's a risk—a big one, in fact—but it may be our only option."

The others nod that they agree.

I sigh and say, "Very well, Your Majesty. If you say so..."

56.

I place a transceiver inside an ornamental brooch, give it to N'Shawn, and instruct him on how it can be used.

"So it's similar to the one I've been wearing even though it's hidden inside the jewelry?" N'Shawn asks.

"That's right. Of course, that makes it not quite as versatile as yours, but it also may allow you to pretend there's something magical about it while talking with K'Shay."

"As far as I'm concerned," he replies, "being able to talk or instantly travel across long distances *is* magic."

"Well, use it however you wish—but I'd prefer for K'Shay not to know too much about me at least until we know where his loyalties lie. In the meantime, we'll send you back to Trojhalter. But be prepared to meet with K'Shay whenever we determine the time is right."

"Understood—and agreed."

*****

That time turns out to be two days later when Bynum (transformed to appear to be Jonnasloan) makes an inspection of both the prison cells under the palace and of the police facilities adjacent to them.

I contact N'Shawn on his transceiver, have him go to a room where he's alone, and then transport him into my quarters on the second floor of the palace. He unlocks and opens the door separating my quarters from the hallway, peeks out, and then uses the key I'd previously given him to lock the door before heading down the stairs and out the front door.

He walks from the palace to the capitol's military barracks, finds K'Shay, and salutes his commander.

"Premander N'Shawn, what are you doing here?" asks K'Shay. "I didn't send for you."

"I know, sir—but an emergency has arisen I must discuss with you in private."

"Very well. I'll be with you as soon as I finish talking with Manatar L'Raizzon."

N'Shawn moves away to the far side of the room, and I use the opportunity to tell him where Bynum is at the moment. When K'Shay finishes with L'Raizzon, he turns to N'Shawn and says, "All right, soldier. What is it you want?"

"I must show you two things here in Van Seissling you need to know about."

"Very well. If you think it's important enough to come all the way from Trojhalter, I'll take the time to see what you have."

"First, you need to tell King Jonnasloan you may have to go to Trojhalter with me. Whether you actually do go is not the point. What is important is that the king thinks you may be going."

K'Shay looks quizzically at N'Shawn and asks, "Really? What's the point?"

"You'll see after I show you the second thing."

"All right. I respect your judgment," K'Shay says with a sigh as he starts to walk toward the palace.

"Not that way, sir. The king is at the police headquarters right now."

"How would you know that?"

"Trust me. I know—and I think you'll understand it all much better shortly."

I continue to keep N'Shawn updated on Bynum's current location as they walk to the police headquarters so that they are able to go directly to where the pretended king is. K'Shay salutes and says, "Sire, something has come up that may require me to go with N'Shawn to Trojhalter."

"No problem. If you do go, just put your troops under your next ranking officer before leaving."

"Will do, Sire. Thank you."

The two soldiers turn and leave the building.

"Come with me," N'Shawn says as he leads K'Shay to the palace. They climb the stairs to the second floor, and N'Shawn uses my key to open the door to my office. They go inside, lock the door, and N'Shawn pulls the brooch out of his pocket. "Magic brooch," he says, "take us to the real King Jonnasloan."

Vicky immediately transports both men into the room where Jonnasloan is lying on a bed in his undergarments, unconscious.

"What in the world?" exclaims K'Shay.

"This is the real Jonnasloan," says N'Shawn. "The man wearing his clothes and pretending to be him is actually in league with the demons that killed our soldiers at Lake Zaragon."

"How do you know about that?"

"I'll tell you later. Right now we've got to get out of here before the demon pretending to be King Jonnasloan returns. Help me pick up the real Jonnasloan."

As they lift the unconscious ruler, N'Shawn says, "Magic brooch, take us back to Wizard Max's quarters." Vicky immediately transports all three men to my bedroom on the second floor of the palace.

"I don't have much time," N'Shawn tells K'Shay, "since I have to get the real King Jonnasloan out of here before the demon pretending to be him returns. Listen carefully and I'll tell you the most important stuff quickly before I go.

"The man pretending to be king is using a transformation potion to make him look and sound like the real King Jonnasloan. Since a necessary ingredient is Jonnasloan's blood, removing Jonnasloan from the demons' control cuts off their ability to make new potion. Once their available potion runs out, which will probably be in just a few days, the demons will probably have to come up with another substitution kinda like they did before with King Kylandar."

"Wait! They did this earlier with Kylandar?"

"That's right. The demons kidnapped him and put Jonnasloan on the throne. Jonnasloan agreed to allow the demons to exit Abaddon and pass through Ventryvia in exchange for being named king. He wanted that power in order to help solve some of our country's problems. When he discovered the demons were making the problems worse, he tried to rescind the agreement. That's when the demons put him under this spell but let him live so they could use his blood for the transformation potion.

"Here, take this brooch and keep it with you at all times. If you need to escape or go someplace, tell the brooch where you need to go and it can probably take you there."

"Probably?"

"Yeah. It's magic—but the magic has its limits. There are some places it might not be able to take you. I don't know how long the magic will hold out, but it's been good for over a year now. This is the way we were able to get our troops into Van Seissling last year to defeat Wizard Malmortiken."

"Really? So that's how you did it."

"Yep. And with this brooch, you now have that power."

"Thanks, N'Shawn. I appreciate your entrusting me with this."

"Well, you're the commander of our armies now, sir—so it should be yours. I do, however, need to use it one last time to take Jonnasloan to a safer place."

"Of course."

"And then you'll need to use it to get outside this room without unlocking the door."

"Oh . . . I—I guess that's right."

N'Shawn gathers Jonnasloan into his arms and says, "Magic brooch, take King Jonnasloan and me to the safe house prepared for him."

Vicky immediately transports them to a tent that has been set up next to the lake in Hidden Canyon, where they are met by Jenny, who has agreed to feed and take care of her master while he remains under the spell placed on him by Count DeVil.

57.

"The prison cells should work nicely as holding areas," Bynum says into his enchanted mirror while talking to Count DeVil.

"Good. I was hoping that would be the case," DeVil replies. "When is your wife joining you at the palace?"

"She's planning on coming tomorrow."

"Good to hear. Let me know when she arrives. And keep me posted on any other developments."

"Will do, boss."

Bynum clicks off the mirror and puts it back into his desk drawer. He stretches while standing up, pushes back his chair, and ambles toward the guest room. He opens the door, starts to walk inside, and freezes in place as he sees the empty bed.

"What the—" Bynum mutters while drawing a knife from its sheath on his belt. Holding the knife in attack position, he carefully examines all parts of the guest room. Then he explores the rest of the suite of rooms but is unable to find Jonnasloan anywhere.

Bynum checks his image in the mirror attached to his closet door to make certain he still appears to be King Jonnasloan before opening the front door to his suite of rooms and asking Fitzroy, "Did anyone go in or out of this office while I was inspecting the police quarters and cells?"

"No, sire."

"Were you there at your desk the entire time?"

"Yes, sire."

"And you saw and heard nothing?"

"I was sitting at my desk the entire time you were gone. I was wide awake and saw and heard nothing out of the ordinary. And no one went in or out of your office while you were gone."

Bynum closes the door and searches all the rooms of his suite before sitting down at his desk and taking his enchanted mirror from its drawer.

"Scrymarron Count DeVil."

After a moment DeVil's voice answers, "What do you want?"

"Jonnasloan's disappeared."

"What?"

"While I was inspecting the police building and prison cells, he disappeared. I've searched all my rooms and he's just not here. Could his spell have worn off?"

"No. Not that spell. Could someone have rescued him?"

"Fitzroy swears that no one went in or out of my offices while I was gone."

"Hold on. I'll be there as quickly as I can."

Bynum puts away his mirror, walks to his front door, and asks Fitzroy, "Do you remember Count DeVil?"

"Yes, sire,"

"He's on his way to see me. When he gets here, just let him come on in without announcing him."

"Yes, sire."

58.

"You've already fully searched all these rooms, haven't you?" Count DeVil asks Bynum upon arriving at the palace.

"Yes sir. Three times."

DeVil spreads his arms wide and commands, "Resplandarex Jonnasloan!"

Both men walk through the king's suite of rooms but Jonnasloan's not there. DeVil opens the door to the king's balcony, steps back, and says, "Xandangelo Jonnasloan." When the balcony and walls turn blue, the Count shakes his head. "He didn't escape this direction. I want to question your secretary."

"Fitzroy? I'll get him."

As Bynum returns with his secretary, DeVil points to the doors. They shut and lock themselves.

Fitzroy jumps, regains his composure, and asks the Count, "You wished to see me, sir?"

"Yes, Fitzroy. Have a seat." DeVil makes a slight motion with his hands and a chair moves from across the room to catch Fitzroy as he is flung backward into it. "I'm going to ask you a few questions and it is imperative that you answer truthfully and completely. Do you understand?"

"Yes sir."

"Who entered the king's chambers while he was gone?"

"No one, sir."

"Who left the king's chambers while he was gone?'

"No one, sir."

"Perhaps you did not understand how imperative it is to answer truthfully and completely," DeVil says while grasping Fitzroy's left arm. Fitzroy's eyes widen in alarm as his left sleeve smolders and then catches on fire. DeVil releases the arm and the fire is immediately extinguished—but singe marks remain.

"Let's try again. Answer the questions again, Fitzroy, but this time be more truthful and complete."

"I was being truthful and complete, sir. I was wide awake at my desk the entire time King Jonnasloan was out of his office inspecting the prison and police facilities. No one entered his suite of rooms and no one left them."

"Is that your final answer?"

"If you want me to be truthful and complete, that's the only answer I can give."

Count DeVil sighs and walks over to the cage containing the cicada-scorpion demons. Bending down, he opens the cage door and says, "Hello, pets. Have fun."

The winged demon flies over to Fitzroy and begins stinging him. DeVil lovingly strokes the other demon and new wings instantly regenerate on its body. It then joins its companion.

Count DeVil puts his arm around Bynum's back and says, "Come out onto the balcony with me, my friend, and let's discuss what we need to do next."

59.

I'm awakened from a sound sleep two days later when an alarm goes off in my bedroom. I crawl out of bed, check the alarm, and see that Vicky has an urgent message for me. I push the response button and ask, "What is it?"

"The probes I assigned to the demon army show that the demons have re-entered Ventryvia. There are additional demons coming out of the hole on Wizard's Island in Lake Zaragon."

"Put it on the screens in my office. I'll be there as soon as I put on my clothes and get Kylandar."

When I get to my office, I see that all three screens are displaying images. The left screen displays thousands of humanoid creatures assembled in ranks and files along the edge of a body of water. Although most of them are wearing armor, some are dressed similarly to medieval monks back on Earth. All of them carry blow tubes and have bandoliers of darts draped across their bodies. I watch as two giant flying wolves pull a raft carrying more soldiers to the shore.

"So that's how they're being transported from Wizard's Island," I remark just as Kylandar enters my office.

"What's that?" he asks, and I explain how the soldiers from Abaddon are being carried across Lake Zaragon.

The right screen shows the demons that have previously invaded the land. The gossamer ghost-like demons are skimming near the tops of trees, while the flying monkeys soar above them. I can also make out a cloud of insect-like creatures.

"Is that cloud a swarm of locusts?" I ask Vicky.

"No sir. It's a cloud of demons—what you call cicada-scorpions."

"Where are those things?"

"Look at the center screen. I've charted both armies of demons on a map of Ventryvia."

The demons with blow tubes are still clustered along the south edge of Lake Zaragon, though they have begun their march southward. The other demon armies have crossed the eastern border of Ventryvia and are moving westward. The two groups will probably meet along the Andora River somewhere between Lake Zaragon and the city of Korivan.

"What do you make of that?" I ask Kylandar.

"It appears DeVil and his demons plan to take Ventryvia by force."

"But why? He already controls the throne."

"That's apparently not good enough for him. Think about it, Max. First you rescued me from their prison. Then N'Shawn got Jonnasloan out of their clutches. Once they run out of his blood, they can't continue to make their transformation potion. That means that . . . uh, what's-his-name—"

"Bynum?"

"Yeah, Bynum. That means that Bynum can't continue pretending to be king."

"I'm still surprised they're resorting to force."

"They haven't yet. Who knows for certain what demons have in mind to do? In any event, we need to study their tactics and see if we can spot any weaknesses."

60.

A sarheit rushes up to Premander K'Shay, salutes, and offers him a small rolled up piece of paper. K'Shay returns the salute and asks, "What do you have, soldier?"

"This message was delivered to us by homing hoxum[3] a short while ago. It comes from an outpost near the eastern border of Ventryvia,"

K'Shay takes the note, reads it, and says, "Thank you, soldier. Return to your post. Immediately get me any other messages you receive."

"Yes sir." The sarheit salutes, turns and leaves.

K'Shay turns to his aide and commands, "Sound the alert. Order battle stations. I have to take this message to the king."

A few minutes later Premander K'Shay reports to Bynum, who is still transformed so that he appears to be King Jonnasloan. "Sire, we've received word that the demonic forces that attacked both Korivan and some of our soldiers at Wizard's Island have crossed Ventryvia's eastern border and are headed westward."

The fake king walks to a large wall map of Ventryvia and says, "Show me where they are now."

---

[3] A bird about the size of a hawk but trained to deliver messages similar to homing pigeons on Earth.

"When they passed our outpost about here," K'Shay says while pointing to a spot on the map, "the scout at the outpost sent us a message by homing hoxum. I don't know precisely where they are now, but they were moving in this direction."

Bynum studies the map intently for a few minutes. "They may be heading back to their home in Abaddon. If so, I don't want to block their way or delay their exit. On the other hand, they could be going to Korivan. Those poor people have suffered enough from the earlier demon attacks and don't need additional misery. Gather your troops so that they can form a protective shield around Korivan. Notify me when you're ready to move out and I'll go with you."

61.

K'Shay positioned himself atop a tower overlooking Korivan's main gate. The city was built on the high point above the confluence of the Argandola and Andora Rivers. However, K'Shay's attention is directed in the opposite direction, following the Andora northward toward Lake Zaragon. Somewhere out there a mighty army of demons is gathering. But where? And for what purpose?

A high ridge to the north of Korivan blocks his view. K'Shay pulls the "magic brooch" out of his pocket and fingers it nervously. It transported him and N'Shawn safely to and from Wizard Max's room in the palace. Will it work to successfully take him to the top of that ridge? There's only one way to find out.

"Magic brooch, take me to the top of the ridge in front of me."

He waits, but nothing happens,

"Magic brooch, take me to the top of the high ridge to the north of Korivan."

Still nothing.

"Magic brooch, this is—"

K'Shay's words fail as a tugging at his midsection pulls him into a cold black void that is quickly replaced by a crashing of tree limbs as he finds himself falling through branches. He grabs hold of one. It breaks, but he snares another and is able to stop his fall. After catching his breath and orienting himself, he carefully climbs down out of the tree, creeps through the underbrush to the top of the ridge and examines the landscape.

Since the forest in which he stands slopes gently downward toward the north, K'Shay is able to remain under the shade of the trees while moving quietly forward. The trees suddenly end at the edge of a valley.

In the distance is another high ridge—and moving across it is an army composed of hundreds of humanoid demons carrying blowtubes. A cloud of smaller flying creatures is visible in the air over those troops. And all of them are moving southward toward K'Shay and Korivan.

To the east of the demon army, a gentle fog seems to be seeping through the trees of the forest. As the fog tops a nearby hill and begins a slow descent toward K'Shay, he suddenly realizes why it seems vaguely familiar: It's not really fog but is instead a low-lying cloud of gossamer ghosts like the ones that caused his men to go crazy and start attacking each other at Wizard's Island.

Oh man! I can't let those things get to me.

K'Shay pulls out his brooch and says into it, "Magic brooch, take me back to the tower in Korivan where I had been before you brought me here."

62.

"If the demons are heading south toward us, they obviously are invading Ventryvia rather than leaving it to go back to Abaddon," Bynum says after K'Shay finishes his scouting report. "We need to stop them before they reach Korivan. Deploy your troops in whatever manner you deem best to accomplish that objective."

"Yes, Sire," K'Shay replies. He salutes the fake king and goes back to his soldiers. *He looks and sounds like the real King Jonnasloan. But I helped rescue the real Jonnasloan—so I know this one is an imposter. If he's actually in league with the demons as N'Shawn claims, this could easily be a trap for me and my men. Nevertheless, we've got to follow orders.*

K'Shay considers his options, examines his maps and notes, and then places his best fighters along Korivan's outer wall with the bulk of them along the north side facing the oncoming demonic forces. A company of archers takes its place atop the high ridge K'Shay had used earlier to spy on the advancing demons, and armored warriors with shields and swords are interspaced with the archers and protect their flanks.

From his perch in a tall tower overlooking Korivan's northern wall, K'Shay strains to see what's happening with his troops that are spread out along that ridge, which hides the hordes of demons advancing from the other side. But he suddenly becomes aware of something else that is moving toward him and his troops. A dark cloud is advancing with dreadful swiftness—and it seems to be alive. The dark specks comprising the cloud appear to have wings larger than locusts but smaller than most birds. The sound generated by those wings is like metallic thunder rolling across the land as it advances.

Flying at the front of the cloud of cicada-scorpion demons is a man on a huge black flying wolf. Count DeVil signals to his flying demons and they swoop down on the front lines of Ventryvian soldiers.

Anguished cries arise from men stung by the demons. But K'Shay has prepared his army for such an attack, and armored soldiers step forward and attack the dive-bombing cicada-scorpions with paddles similar in size and shape to skillet frying pans. As the demons are swatted to the ground, they are then stomped by boots and killed with swords and maces.

The soldiers who were stung are escorted back to Korivan, where they are examined by healers who use a variety of magical remedies in an effort to counteract the demons' venom. K'Shay had ordered that they be kept in a secure area where they could be treated and observed.

While the cicada-scorpions attacked from the air, the army of demons armed with blowtubes advanced across the valley toward the Ventryvian archers and swordsmen on the south edge of the valley. Since the demons use their shields to deflect the volleys of arrows fired by the archers, the demonic army has moved relentlessly forward across the valley.

Shouts suddenly ring out across the battlefield. Some are warning cries from demons catching sight of movement on their right flank. Even louder is the battle cry "For Ventryvia and our king!" yelled by armored soldiers riding their sorraks into the demonic forces, using swords and maces to cut swaths through the demonic ranks.

"Like hot knives cutting through lardisone," Requinder M' Kiver says to Requinder L'Raisson as the two officers watch the action unfolding before them.

"Yes. Hiding the mounted troops in the woods along the west flank until the demonic forces were fully committed in the valley was a brilliant tactic. Premander K'Shay is a good commander."

The two requinders watch as the Ventryvian mounted troops slash through the demonic army, reveling in their success so much that they fail to see the ghostly cloud of ethereal spirits floating toward their troops. As each demonic spirit comes in contact with a mounted soldier, the demon disappears as if being absorbed—and then the countenance, conduct and demeanor of the soldier totally changes. Prior to the transformation, he is a fully committed weapon of war fighting for Ventryvia against its demonic enemies. Afterwards, he has become one of those demonic enemies as he turns and fights against any of his comrades who have not yet been possessed and transformed.

As the ghostly cloud sweeps across the battlefield where the front lines of combatants converge, the tide of battle reverses with the demons adding soldiers to their ranks, more than replacing those that had been lost in combat.

"Quick!" M'Kiver yells to L'Raisson. "Get word to Premander K'Shay about what's happening to our troops."

"Will do, sir!" L'Raisson responds as he spurs his sorrak and gallops back through the lines of Ventryvian soldiers.

63.

K'Shay curses as L'Raisson finishes his report, and then turns toward Bynum and asks, "Do you have any questions, Sire?"

"My understanding is that although our troops were initially successful against the demons, the enemy now has gained the advantage. Is that correct?"

"Yes, Sire. That was the situation at the time I left to warn Premander K'Shay."

"What do we do now?" Bynum asks K'Shay.

K'Shay shakes his head but whatever he is about to say is interrupted by a loud commotion from the high ridge to the north of Korivan. All three men turn to look in that direction.

Hundreds of Ventryvian troops, routed from their defensive positions on the other side of the ridge, are suddenly swarming across the ridge, apparently running for their lives. But the forces immediately in pursuit of them are not the demons, but are rather armored Ventryvian soldiers mounted on sorraks, riding through and decimating the ranks of Ventryvian archers and infantry.

"My army is destroying itself!" K'Shay cries in anguish.

"Yes Sir," L'Raisson says. "That's why I rushed here to warn you."

"I understand, but it's still horrible to witness."

The mounted warriors are followed by a vast array of demons carrying blowtubes. Over their heads float clouds of ethereal ghostlike demons apparently searching for new bodies to invade and possess. Although a few dozen Ventryvian soldiers are able to reach the relative safety of Korivan's city walls, demons soon control all the area around Korivan, and no soldiers still loyal to Ventryvia remain alive on the plains outside the city.

Bynum turns to K'Shay and asks, "Are those ghostlike creatures the same as what you said attacked your troops at Lake Zaragon?"

"Yes, Sire. They appear to be the same."

"Only there they caused your men to fight each other—but then they left."

"That's correct. Now they are remaining in the soldiers they have possessed and are using the men as additional demonic troops. I don't know which way is worse."

"But we don't have any defense against them?"

"None that I've found."

"Are they killed or even harmed by any of our weapons?"

"Not that I've seen." K'Shay turns to L'Raisson and asks, "Have you seen anything that can hurt or kill the ghostly demons?"

"No Sir. I haven't."

Both soldiers turn and look at Bynum. He shakes his head, sighs and says, "Then its only a matter of time before they wipe us out. Unless you can immediately come up with a viable alternative, I may have no choice but to surrender."

The three men stand looking at each other for a moment before Bynum tells K'Shay, "Find something white we can use as a flag of truce and meet me at Korivan's main gate."

"Now, Sire?"

"Yes, Premander. Immediately."

64.

K'Shay sits astride his sorrak at the main gate of Korivan. His right hand is wrapped tightly around a flagpole, but the banner unfurled at the top is as blank and unfeeling as the lives of K'Shay's soldiers killed by demonic forces.

K'Shay stares mutely at the white flag that has replaced Ventryvia's colors. It wasn't supposed to end this way. As he had fought his way through battles and worked his way up through the ranks of his country's armies, he had always relished the thrill of victory and feel of success.

Well, *almost* always. Technically, he had been defeated a year ago when he surrendered to King Kylandar. But the only reason he had willingly commanded Wizard Malmortiken's forces was that he feared what the wizard would do to K'Shay's family if he didn't lead the troops in their rebellion. Kylandar's victory didn't particularly feel like a defeat for K'Shay.

But this time is totally different. This time K'Shay must surrender to an army from Abaddon. To demonic forces. To evil incarnate! It is unspeakably wrong—but it also appears to be the only way any of them can survive. The ghostlike apparitions can invade the bodies of his soldiers, possess them, and even take over their actions. None of their weapons have been able to kill those demons, and none of their armor has protected his soldiers from being possessed by the demonic forces.

Bynum—still in the guise of King Jonnasloan—rides up to K'Shay and says, "Let's go." Together they ride out from Korivan, move around the city, and then turn northward toward the demonic army. The hordes of demons are spread out as far as their eyes can see, and the oppressive feel of evil almost overwhelms K'Shay's soul. He finds it hard to breathe, notices that his sorrak appears spooked or skittish, and they momentarily stop in their tracks. But Bynum's sorrak continues ambling forward, so K'Shay spurs his mount ahead to join them.

The ranks of demons part to let them through. Ahead of them is a tent that has been set up. *Are they expecting us? Or is that just where the demons' commanding officer is staying? It could be either—or both.*

Guards step forward and take the reins of both sorraks while other guards keep their weapons pointed at Bynum and K'Shay as they dismount. One of the demons motions for K'Shay to place his weapons on the ground, and he does so. Now both men are unarmed as they are led into the tent. K'Shay passes the white flag to a demon.

Count DeVil rises to meet them. He smiles, makes a slight movement with his hands, and two chairs appear in the space beside them.

"Sit," commands DeVil.

Bynum and K'Shay settle into the chairs.

"What do you want?" asks DeVil.

"We do not desire a war," Bynum answers. "However, you are bringing a large army into our country. Why?"

"The entry portal from Abaddon into your world lies within your borders. You had agreed we could use it before later changing your mind. That portal must remain open to us."

"It must remain open," Bynum repeats in a mechanical voice.

K'Shay glances back and forth between Bynum and DeVil. When the putative king again mutters, "Yes. The portal must remain open," K'Shay leans forward and asks, "And if we refuse?"

DeVil smiles. "You won't refuse." He flicks his right wrist and a gossamer apparition glides into the tent and merges with K'Shay's body.

The military commander suddenly feels a cold sensation somewhat like the empty heartless void of a frozen wilderness. The cold void quickly spreads through his body. Its icy tendrils grip his vital organs, slow his heartbeat and make it difficult to breathe. Then they pulse up into his brain and the icy coldness changes to a warmth and feeling of power like none he has previously experienced. The desire and lust for power and control is an all-consuming hunger that must be fed. It must be satisfied. Nothing else matters. Somehow he also knows that Count DeVil can feed that hunger and help him achieve his goals. He turns to DeVil and smiles. "Yes, I see what you mean. What else do you want?"

"Just one other thing, and I think you'll like it. I'd like us to combine forces under your leadership."

"You mean I'll command both Ventryvia's armies and your demons?"

"That's right. Well, you'd still be under your king—but otherwise . . ."

K'Shay sits back and thinks. He has often felt the satisfaction of seeing enemies fall before him—and that was when he was merely wielding his own strength and the power of mortal forces. How much greater would be the power if he also had supernatural forces under his command?

"Ooooh. We'll be invincible."

"That's the idea, my friend. That's the idea."

65.

"What's happening now?" Kylandar asks as he walks into my office.

"I'm not sure," I respond. "Bynum and K'Shay are riding to DeVil's tent under a white flag of truce. Vicky, is K'Shay's transceiver turned on?"

"Yes, sir—but the sound is not very clear, since its hidden inside jewelry you called a 'magic brooch'—and that jewelry is stuffed inside a pocket. I'll record it and enhance whatever I can for you."

"Thank you."

We watch as the two men are escorted into Count DeVil's tent. Since we don't have a probe inside the tent, we are unable to snoop on their meeting, though I hope Vicky will be able to salvage enough speech from the "magic brooch" to give us ample warning of what might be about to happen.

Bynum and K'Shay eventually emerge from the tent, get back onto their sorraks, and ride back to Korivan.

"Address your troops and then have them return to Van Seissling," Bynum tells K'Shay before retiring to his quarters.

"Yes, sire." K'Shay then calls his top subcommanders to him. I move a flying probe closer to the group.

"This entire confrontation was apparently the result of a misunderstanding between King Jonnasloan and Count DeVil, who is apparently the High Lord or Prince of Abaddon. King Jonnasloan had earlier agreed to allow Abaddon's forces free entry and passage through Ventryvia but did not realize we were supposed to keep the entry portal clear. When we obstructed the portal with some of our soldiers, those soldiers were killed—which led to this conflict. Both sides now have a clearer understanding of the agreement. In fact, we've even agreed to work together on some things, which should help us in the future."

"Excuse me, sir," says Requinder M'Kiver. "Request permission to speak freely, sir."

"Go ahead, Requinder."

"Does this mean Ventryvian forces will be under the control of Abaddon demons?"

"No, Requinder. Actually, it will be the opposite way. Jonnasloan will continue to be king of Ventryvia, and I will command both our forces and those that join us from Abaddon."

"Thank you, sir. That makes me feel better."

"If you have no other questions, gather our troops and return to Van Seissling. King Jonnasloan has a few things he needs me to do before I join you there."

"Yes, sir."

66.

"Sir," Vicky says through my transceiver. "K'Shay has just instructed the "magic brooch" to take him to Trojhalter."

"Then do it—but make certain there are at least one or two probes nearby and put their transmissions onto my screens."

"Yes, sir. And I'm still processing those other recordings for you. It's hard to enhance recordings that are so dim and muffled."

"Thanks. Let me hear them when you finish."

*****

Kylandar, Rhylene and I watch as K'Shay is transported into N'Shawn's presence in Trojhalter.

"Good afternoon, Premander N'Shawn. Where did you take King Jonnasloan?"

"Some place where he'll probably be safe from the demons . . . as long as not many people know where that place is."

"I agree with your reasoning, but the situation has changed."

"What's happened?"

"Abaddon's forces invaded Ventryvia. Our military is good against mortals but not against supernatural demons. They were wiping us out until we called a truce and negotiated a peace settlement that left us in control."

"Oh?"

"We agreed not to block their portal to our world through Wizard's Island, but otherwise everything remains the same. Ventryvia is still ruled by our king and I remain as head of our armed forces."

"But sir, we aren't really being ruled by *our* king. King Kylandar was removed by demonic force and one of their demons is now pretending to be King Jonnasloan."

"That's true, but we can't afford either a panic or a rebellion at this time. The demons are too strong and would wipe us out. Quite frankly, we are fortunate to still have our country and to be in control."

"But are we really still in control if a demon sits on our throne and runs the country as our king?"

K'Shay's expression freezes and he simply stares at N'Shawn momentarily. Then some kind of ghostlike entity seems to pass out of his body and enter into N'Shawn, who shivers.

N'Shawn's body shakes a few times and then his head also shakes. His expression changes and he says, "Yes, I think I understand what you are saying. You think the people don't have to know that we now have a different king. It's more important that we avoid a panic or anything else that would give the demons an excuse to totally overrun our country. What you say makes sense, sir."

K'Shay smiles, steps forward and puts his right hand on N'Shawn's left shoulder. "Just follow orders and we'll make it through these trying times all right."

N'Shawn again shivers, he appears somewhat confused, but doesn't say anything. Instead, the two commanders merely salute each other before K'Shay says, "Magic brooch, take me back to my quarters in Korivan."

67.

"What do you make of that?" Kylandar asks me.

"Well, sire, N'Shawn seems willing to help K'Shay avoid a popular uprising or panic."

"But why?"

"It could be any of several things: Chain of command coupled with orders from a superior officer; free will overridden by demonic control; desire not to reveal too much data to K'Shay or the demons. Take your choice. Or it might be none of them—or some combination of them. I thought I saw a ghostlike shape float over from K'Shay to N'Shawn before he agreed help K'Shay."

"I thought I saw that, too," Kylandar says.

"Me too," adds Rhylene. "And I thought I later saw it return to K'Shay."

"I didn't see that part," I say. "Vicky, if you recorded that exchange between the two military commanders, put it on screen for us to review."

"Yes sir," Vicky says and puts it on my central monitor, playing the last part a second time in slow motion.

"Yeah, you're right, Rhylene," I say. "A gossamer apparition enters N'Shawn until he agrees to help, and then it returns to K'Shay."

"What was that thing, anyway?"

"It looked the way I remember the ghostlike demons at Lake Zaragon when they caused our soldiers to kill one another."

"But neither K'Shay nor N'Shawn became belligerent or threatening," Rhylene says.

"No, but they may still have been under its control—" I break off my sentence as the transceiver in my left ear informs me, "Call from N'Shawn."

I turn toward the others and say, "We may be about to find out. N'Shawn is calling me." I hit the "receive" switch and say, "This is Max."

"Max, N'Shawn here. Premander K'Shay wants to know where I took Jonnasloan. I was able to get by without telling him the actual location, but I think I may have agreed to help him avoid public panic by allowing the demons to run the country. What should I do?"

"What do you want to do?"

"Well, he's my commanding officer and may be wanting to gain possession of Jonnasloan. On the other hand, we went to a lot of effort to get Jonnasloan away from them."

"Did you agree to assist him?"

"I think so. My mind seemed confused and clouded toward the end of our talk."

"Why would you agree?"

"Partly because it was an order from my commander and partly because it seemed to be the most expedient course of action—but I think there was something else as well."

"What?"

Well, I hate to admit it, but I think I may have been momentarily possessed by demonic forces."

"Tell me about it—in full and with any details you can remember. This could be vitally important for us to know."

"Yes sir; I'll try. I was trying to figure out how I could refuse or deflect what I thought he was about to ask me to do. As I looked at Premander K'Shay, something seemed to come out of his body and float toward me. I started shivering as a cold void spread through my body. I could feel my heartbeat slow, I had trouble breathing, and I feared I might be about to die. Then I started warming up, my brain felt hot as if I was getting heat stroke, and I suddenly felt all powerful. I had a sudden urge to do anything K'Shay told me to do, whether or not it was a command—as if all my objections had been satisfactorily answered. Whatever it was that had entered me promised me things no one else could give me—freedom from my burdens of responsibility and conscience. I could imagine closing my eyes with no worries, no pain, no hunger, no regrets and no guilt. It was a weird feeling, but enough of the feeling of warmth and power remained even after K'Shay left that I now have a gnawing hunger to regain the sense of power that I momentarily possessed. I sat still thinking about it for a while before contacting you."

I look at Kylandar and Rhylene before answering N'Shawn in my transceiver, "Are you still willing to help King Kylandar reclaim his throne?"

"Yes, of course. That hasn't changed."

"What if K'Shay opposes you?"

"That would make it more difficult, since I would be disobeying an order from my commanding officer—but if King Kylandar gives me an order, then I shouldn't be guilty of treason for following my king's order."

"Keep in touch. I'll get back with you."

I turn off my transceiver, glance at Kylandar and ask, "What do you think?"

"I think that thing—whatever it is—seems to at least partially take over the person it enters. It initially felt cold to N'Shawn, but then it apparently altered his feelings and thoughts."

"And when it exited his body, it left him hungry."

"Hungry for what?" asks Rhylene.

"Hungry for power; hungry for its presence," I answer. "Have we lost N'Shawn to the demons, or can we still trust him?"

"Oh, I trust him," Kylandar says, "and he apparently still trusts me and considers me to be his king. But the demons' ability to enter people and do crazy things with their minds is scary."

"Yeah," I agree. "What makes it even scarier is that they aren't killed by our weapons. Those creatures weren't phased by anything our soldiers have done."

"Is there any way we can stop them?" Rhylene asks.

"I don't know of anything," her father replies. "But we can't let them overrun the country unopposed. We have to do something."

"But what?" she asks,

The three of us just look at each other, but no one has an answer.

68.

I have Vicky play and replay the various recordings of our soldiers' encounters with the ghostlike demons. They caused the soldiers to attack and kill each other at Lake Zaragon—but then departed, leaving behind the dead bodies. They took possession of the warriors outside Korivan and caused them to fight against their Ventryvian comrades.

Since swords and arrows don't harm them, I can't think of any Ventryvian weapon that can defeat them. *Is there any weapons on my spacecraft that would be effective?* I mentally run through our inventory and conclude there's nothing we possess that could probably work.

I again watch the conversation between K'Shay and N'Shawn. *Kylandar's right: It **is** scary how those demons can take possession of people's minds and make them do crazy things.*

I next have Vicky show me current scenes from our probes in and around Korivan. *There must be some weakness the demons have that we can exploit—some way we can attack them.* But I can't find anything.

"What are you looking at?" Kylandar asks as he enters my office.

"Korivan," I tell him. "Maybe I'm being naive or forgetful, but I don't remember there being this much crime, violence and rowdiness prior to the demons' invasion."

Kylandar turns and studies the screens for a few minutes. "Yeah," he agrees. "It's not unusual for there to be rowdiness and fighting going on in Korivan. But what we're seeing here seems a bit much—especially in broad daylight.

"Whoa! Look at this over here." Kylandar hops up and points to the right screen, where several couples, threesomes and foursomes are attempting to disrobe one another and engage in various sexual activities. They seem to have abandoned their inhibitions and moral restraints and are instead intent on feeding their most basic physical hungers and desires.

I turn to Kylandar and remark, "I don't think I've seen this level of public lewdness in broad daylight previously."

"I suspect demons have caused them to lose their moral compass, Max. The cesspool continues to deepen and expand."

"Do you think the demons are at least partially responsible?"

"Almost certainly. We've got to do something, Max."

"What?"

"I don't know. If I knew our weapons were effective against them, I'd say we need to counterattack with our armed forces. But we haven't been able to harm or even touch those ghost-like demons. You might look through Malmortiken's magic scrolls to see if you can find anything that could work. We've got to do something—and quickly."

*****

Although I took over Wizard Malmortiken's old offices and sleeping quarters at the palace and now own (and sometimes read or study) his scrolls containing magical spells and incantations, I don't pretend to be a magician or know much about the fields of magic that seem to pervade this planet. Granted, the technology I brought with me from Earth and my training and tools as an engineer are viewed as being magical by the people of Ventryvia, but I'd be as lost as a little kitten in strange surroundings if I tried to use Malmortiken's magic.

Instead, I set aside several extra hours for prayer and Bible study over and above the time I normally use for prayer, quiet time, and devotions. The 91st Psalm assures me that I can trust God as my refuge and fortress, since he will save me from my enemies and from deadly pestilence: *A thousand may fall at your side, ten thousand at your right hand, but it will not come near you. You will only observe with your eyes and see the punishment of the wicked. If you make the Most High your dwelling, then no harm will befall you.*

I kneel down and pray, "Oh Lord, please let this be your promise and not just a poem or song. I don't know how we can defeat demonic or supernatural forces of evil apart from your hand and provision. Please lead, guide and direct us—and let me know whether to step out in faith or to wait for a more definite word or sign from you."

I crawl into bed and try to fall to sleep—but sleep eludes me. When it finally does come, I am rewarded with the most vivid dream I can recall occurring during my life. The colors are unbelievably bright and beautiful. Light pervades everything. The air is crystal clear. Sunlight glints off numberless prisms, shattering the light rays, deflecting them, reflecting them so dazzlingly that I am overwhelmed by the prismatic light.

Bathed in the luster of that light, even the leaves of the trees and blades of grass shine forth with special glory. And the flowers are masterpieces of beauty. It's as if each object is radiating its own light—as if that beautiful prismatic light is coming from inside each leaf, each petal, each part of everything I see.

I am seeing in a manner I have never before seen. It's as if something has been stripped from my eyes—as if I have heretofore been seeing through a glass darkly, but now can see all things face to face.

And the face that I see is of a man I don't recognize. His face is strong and commanding, but also trustworthy and welcoming. He beckons me to follow him and I gladly do so. He draws his sword, and it gleams with unnatural light. We're flying now. I didn't know I had wings or could fly, but I have to follow him as he leads his mighty host of angels into battle.

Angels? Battle?

I suddenly wake up. It's morning. I lie half-dazed for a few minutes before climbing out of bed. I accidently knock my Bible off the small table next to my bed. It falls open to the first chapter of Joshua. My eyes fall upon the scripture that says *I will be with you; I will never leave you nor forsake you. . . .Be strong and courageous! Do not be afraid or discouraged. For the Lord your God is with you wherever you go.*

69.

I shower, shave, get dressed, and walk to the kitchen. Kylandar is already there. I ask him, "Are you ready to lead your troops against the demons?"

"I don't know where the troops are, but I'm more than ready to lead them."

"In that case, let's get the troops."

Kylandar nods his assent.

"Vicky," I say, "patch me through to N'Shawn."

When N'Shawn answers, I tell him our plans and ask how many of the troops at Trojhalter are totally loyal to Kylandar.

"The Dragon Company and King's Regiment troops that have been under my command for years are totally loyal. I think they'd follow King Kylandar and me anywhere under any conditions and against any odds. The other troops here would probably follow my orders. However, if my orders were countermanded by Premander K'Shay and the man pretending to be king, I really couldn't say what they'd do."

"If you'll assemble your soldiers, King Kylandar and I can address them."

"Will do, sir."

70.

Two days later Kylandar, N'Shawn and I lead our troops toward Korivan. My probes have shown us that although K'Shay has sent the bulk of the Ventryvian army back to Van Seissling, the demonic army is still in and around Korivan. K'Shay has also remained in Korivan in order to meet and assimilate the demonic forces. He seems excited and euphoric about being able to lead them into battle.

We still don't know of any way we can overcome the ghostly apparitions that can enter the bodies of mortals and possess their minds. Nevertheless, we are committed to making a stand against them.

As we crest a ridge, we see the forces under K'Shay's command spread out before us under a sky that's becoming increasingly cloudy. Scouts from both armies have already encountered each other, of course, and I have watched videos of the deployment of forces transmitted by my probes to Vicky on my spacecraft and then relayed to my computer tablet.

Since N'Shawn and K'Shay know and respect each other, they have sent messages via scouts that they wish to meet to discuss matters prior to any potential conflict.

"I'm going with you," Kylandar says, "and I'd like Max to come as well."

N'Shawn and I both nod our approval, and we move forward together on our sorraks. K'Shay and an aide ride toward us from their army and we meet in an open field about halfway between the two opposing forces.

K'Shay rides up to N'Shawn and asks, "Why are you bringing your troops from Trojhalter in battle gear and formation?"

"We're here to assist you in getting rid of the demons, sir."

"I didn't send for these troops. In fact, I specifically told you that the king had negotiated an agreement with the demons that resolved our conflict with them."

"But the man pretending to be king is actually one of the demons. That so-called agreement allows the demons to freely enter Ventryvia and to control the country."

"As your commanding officer, I order you to stand down and return to Trojhalter with your troops."

Kylandar opens his visor so that his face can be seen and recognized. "And as your king and commander, I order you to cease your alliance with demonic forces. Join us and help us defeat them."

K'Shay appears surprised and is momentarily at a loss for words other than exclaiming, "King Kylandar!" He stutters a bit and then says, "Uh . . . It's good to see you again, sire."

"It's good to see you too, K'Shay. But it will be even better if you do what I say."

"I'd like to, sire. I've always liked and respected you, but I'm afraid you don't fully understand the situation."

"What do you mean?"

"We must face reality—and the reality of the situation is that we can't defeat the demons. I threw everything we had at them. We could kill the small insect-like demons and the humanistic ones, but our weapons had no effect on the ghostly apparitions. Arrows and swords passed through them without hurting them. On the other hand, they can enter our men and take over their bodies and their actions. There's nothing we can do that has any power over them. We were fortunate to be able to work out the agreement to work with them, since that at least stopped the carnage."

"I'm sorry Abaddon's forces killed some of your soldiers, K'Shay, but there's no way I can agree to a partnership with demonic evil or accept one of them as king of Ventryvia."

"I understand your sentiment, sire—and I felt the same way until I watched my men being slaughtered, knowing that none of our weapons stood a chance against those demons. Only a fool would attempt to stand in their way."

"Are you calling me a fool?"

"I've never thought of you in those terms—but you must judge yourself. Is it foolish to deliberately fight against an enemy you know you can't defeat—especially after you've seen how ineffective your weapons are against them?

"So you refuse to join us in opposing the demons?"

"As I said, only a fool would knowingly fight them. I'm not a fool. I'm a realist. I must abide by the agreement we've made with them."

"No, what you must do is to comply with your king's orders—and I've told you to help us destroy the demons. Refusing to do so is treason."

"But are you still king? My orders come from the man currently serving as Ventryvia's king. And in any event, we have met here under flag of truce."

N'Shawn moves forward and says, "But you're marrying yourself to evil demonic forces."

K'Shay smiles wryly. "No, what I've actually done is to join an invincible force. You should come with me, N'Shawn. You have no idea how exhilarating it is to lead an army that can't be defeated. Think about it. Don't oppose me and my unbeatable ghosts. Face reality . . . and stay alive."

We each sit on our sorraks looking at one another without saying anything for several moments—but it becomes obvious that neither side will budge from its position. Then we slowly disengage, turn around, and head back the way we've come.

71.

"I hate the thought of killing Ventryvia's own soldiers," Kylandar says to us as we ride back to our own troops.

"Yeah," N'Shawn agrees. "Many of them are soldiers I've commanded."

"You might not have to," I say. "At least not initially. Take a look at how K'Shay has his troops arranged." I pass my computer tablet to them. Most of his soldiers are humanoid demons carrying blowtubes and darts. Ventryvian knights and infantry are on each side, while archers are at the rear—but the total number of Ventryvian troops are less than the demons with blowtubes.

"Where are the rest of our country's soldiers?" N'Shawn asks.

"They went back to Van Seissling," I reply, "and they haven't returned yet."

"Will they make it back here in time to fight us?"

"Not unless the battle lasts a long time. My probes show that they're still in Van Seissling. Right, Vicky?"

"Yes, sir," Vicky replies in my transceiver. "But there's someone who wants to meet with you at the edge of the forest on your right."

I glance that direction and see someone standing by some trees, but can't make out who it is from this distance. I tell Kylandar and N'Shawn I'll be back shortly, leave my tablet with them, and ride toward the man. As I get closer to him, he walks toward me and I recognize him as being the man I saw in my dream or vision.

"Who are you?" I ask.

"I go by a number of names and titles, but you may call me Michael."

"Michael? The archangel?"

A hint of a smile creases his lips. "You have been praying earnestly about the situation here. The one calling himself Count DeVil has overstepped his bounds. Consequently, I have been permitted to appear to you and to partially open your eyes."

"What do you mean when you say 'partially open my eyes'?"

"Since we operate in a supernatural dimension, people normally can't see us. Your eyes have been partially opened to the supernatural so that you can see me and talk with me. None of the others here can see me or my forces, and you won't see everything. Just know that your prayers have been heard. Follow the directions you will receive."

Michael nods at me once and then disappears as completely as if he had never been there. I stand for a moment or two blinking into the empty void where he had been. Then I return to my companions.

72.

As the opposing armies move toward each other and assume their respective battle positions, the wind picks up and the clouds drop low and begin a threatening rotation. It appears as if a supercell is forming. The bottoms of the clouds bulge like boiling water, and large hailstones pelt the army of demons. Lightning strikes with an intensity I've never seen before—both from the clouds above and from the ground around the demons. The flashes are so spectacularly bright that it's difficult to watch, but I'm reasonably certain that I also see the bright glow of swords being wielded by angelic hosts striking down their demonic foes.

I hear the buzzing of metallic wings and look up. A dark cloud of millions of demonic cicada-scorpions is emerging from the forests beyond Korivan. There's too many of them for us to fight—but not too many for Michael's angels. I really can't tell whether I'm watching lightning or supernatural swords, but the electrocution of those flying demons is truly a sight to behold! The electricity flowing between the millions of tiny bodies is as bright as the sun; it's so bright that I have to look away even though I desperately want to continue watching.

K'Shay had boasted of how euphoric he felt when leading an unbeatable army of demonic ghosts who are not fazed by the arrows, swords or other weapons his Ventryvian troops used against them. I shudder as I watch a cloud of them floating toward us. And then I wonder what K'Shay's thoughts must be as he watches his "invincible" ghostly apparitions be torn asunder by heavenly lightning and supernatural swords.

However, I'm not sure K'Shay actually saw what happened, for when I look to where he had been, I see that he and his sorrak are lying on the ground. One of his officers is examining him. Now that officer stands up, looks around, and then retrieves a white cloth from somewhere and begins waiving it, signaling surrender.

Our army moves forward with Kylandar and N'Shawn in the lead. Although I see the bodies of a few Ventryvian soldiers, almost all of the fallen are the battered remnants of what had been a mighty demonic army.

Kylandar moves his sorrak next to mine, leans over and asks, "Is this the result of your magic?"

"What makes you think that?"

"It seems strange to me that the violent hail and lightning storm so precisely targeted demons while leaving our forces alone."

"That was rather nice of the storm to do that, wasn't it?"

"Too nice. What actually happened, Max?"

"As you saw, it was a rather violent storm with deadly hail and lightning."

"I saw that part. What I want to know is how and why it was directed so precisely against our enemies."

"I think heavenly forces used the storm to destroy demons that had overstepped their bounds."

"Overstepped their bounds?"

"Yes, Your Majesty. Those demons were supposed to remain confined in Abaddon."

Kylandar sits on his sorrak just staring at me without speaking. Then he nods and slowly rides over to where N'Shawn is examining K'Shay's lifeless body.

73.

Kylandar and N'Shawn remain in Korivan overnight, visiting with the troops there and making certain they are loyal to King Kylandar. As nearly as I can tell, the only ones dying in the supernatural storm were the demons and those Ventryvians who had been possessed by them. K'Shay's death leaves N'Shawn as the highest-ranking officer in Ventryvia's army.

I have Vicky transport me back to Hidden Canyon. Rhylene already knows how the battle turned out, since she watched it unfold on the monitors in my office. However, she has a few questions that I attempt to answer before retiring to my bedroom for evening devotions and sleep.

I am awakened during the night by an unnatural glow in my room—and realize the glow is coming from Michael and the sword that hangs at his side.

"Don't be afraid," he says to me. "I know you, your friends, and your troops are planning to confront Bynum and possibly DeVil."

"That's right."

"You are the only mortal on this planet who might have a chance against them."

"Why me? I'm not a warrior or even trained in battle."

"Since Bynum and DeVil are demonic lords, physical weapons won't have any effect on them. Spiritual force must be used."

Michael draws his sword and it glows in the darkness with supernatural fire. "Angelic forces vanquish our foes using soulfire."

"Soulfire?"

"Yes. You saw the high amount of energy that was transmitted from our swords, didn't you?"

"All that lightning and electricity? Yeah."

"That's soulfire. It's strong enough to destroy all but the lords of the demons."

"But you said Bynum and DeVil are demonic lords."

"Right. So soulfire won't kill them—but it can cast them out."

"Cast them out?"

"They don't belong in Ventryvia. Use soulfire to confine them where they belong: In Abaddon."

"But I don't have any soulfire."

"On the contrary. You're the only mortal in Ventryvia who does have it."

"I don't understand."

"God's Holy Spirit has indwelled you ever since you surrendered your life to God when you were nine years old."

"Yeah, but that's different from this soulfire you're talking about. Isn't it?"

"Different—but related. As long as the Holy Spirit indwells you, you have a supernatural power that includes using soulfire."

"If you say so. But I don't have a clue as to how to do it."

Michael unhooks a small scabbard from his belt, opens it, and takes out a knife, which he hands to me. "This knife is made from the same material as angels' swords. It will help you direct your soulfire to the desired object."

"Are you giving this to me?"

"Yes. I just did. Use it well." He also hands me the scabbard.

"Wow! Thank you."

"One word of caution. Soulfire is powerful in the spiritual realm, but it doesn't make you physically invincible. It won't keep your physical body from being injured or killed."

74.

The next morning I sit in my office and watch Kylandar and N'Shawn lead the King's Regiment out of Korivan along the road to Van Seissling. Then I have Vicky show me what's happening at the palace. Bynum is sitting behind the desk in the king's office. He is no longer disguised to look like Jonnasloan. I don't know whether he still has any transformation potion or whether the blood in whatever potion he may have is still fresh enough to work.

Bynum doesn't give any indication that he's aware of the loss of his demonic army at Korivan or that Kylandar and N'Shawn are on their way to Van Seissling. Nevertheless, I find that I am fearful and hesitant to confront him—but I know I must do so. And it would be less dangerous to do it while Count DeVil is not there.

I check my blaster and Michael's knife for the umpteenth time, give Rhylene a goodbye hug, and reluctantly walk out to the meadow, giving Vicky final instructions on the way. Since we have the coordinates for Kylandar's personal office, I have Vicky transport me there.

Bynum appears startled as I materialize directly in front of his desk. He jumps to his feet and draws his sword—and I have a sickening feeling as I realize his sword is a much more formidable weapon than my little knife. I therefore pull out my blaster and shoot him in his chest near his right shoulder.

Bynum swings his sword at me while lunging forward and shouting some word I don't recognize. I duck out of the way and almost don't see the ghostly apparition before it enters my body. I suddenly feel extremely cold and clammy, I start shivering, my heartbeat slows, and I have trouble breathing. *Am I dying?* I don't know. I feel cold and confused. Bynum has moved around the desk and is raising his sword to strike me down.

He suddenly rocks backward on his heels, drops his sword while putting both hands around his head, and lets out a loud yell of pain. As Bynum stumbles backward, my body purges itself of the ghostly apparition and returns to normal. I draw Michael's knife from its scabbard and mentally will my soulfire to banish Bynum from Ventryvia. The knife flashes with a brilliance I wouldn't have believed was possible, the bright light surrounds a very surprised Bynum, and he simply disappears. I stand gaping at the empty spot where he had been standing.

I walk through the suite of rooms, open the door to the hallway, and look out. Tybatha is sitting at the receptionist's desk. She turns to look at me, lets out a surprised squawk, and starts to jump up. I again use the knife to direct my soulfire at her and banish her to Abaddon.

"Vicky," I say into my transceiver, "Do you see Count DeVil or any of the other demons in or around the palace?"

"No sir. Our probes do not detect any."

"What about in Van Seissling?"

"There might be some, but none are showing up—and the same can be said for elsewhere in Ventryvia."

"Thank you. Where are Kylandar and the troops?"

"They should arrive at Van Seissling in about an hour."

"Thanks, Vicky. Keep me posted on anything I need to know."

"Yes, sir. Will do."

I walk through the king's suite of rooms but find nothing that needs to be attended to. Then I go down to my rooms on the second floor of the palace and examine them. Finally, I leave the palace, walk to the royal stables, and have the groom saddle Snowblaze. I ride Snowblaze through town to the front gates of Van Seissling, where I dismount and visit with the soldiers there while waiting for Kylandar, N'Shawn and the King's Regiment.

When they arrive, I bow before King Kylandar and say, "Welcome, Your Majesty. I brought Snowblaze for you to ride in your triumphant return to your throne."

"What about Bynum?"

"He and his wife have been banished to Abaddon. I'll tell you about it when we get to the palace."

If you enjoyed *Kings and Vagabonds,*
Read on for a preview of the next thrilling
Max Strider novel by Bill Kincaid:

1.

As word spread among the citizens of Ventryvia that King Kylandar had returned, they came out of their shops and homes, lined the street leading to the palace, and wildly cheered him as he passed by at the head of his troops. When he arrived at the palace, Kylandar dismounted from Snowblaze, waved to the cheering throngs, and entered the building accompanied by Max Strider, an engineer whom the king considered to be both a friend and his wizard.

Kylandar looked at the people gathered inside the palace, waved to them, and then walked over to Allox, the country's treasurer.

"Are you still fulfilling your duties as treasurer, Allox?" he asked.

"Yes, sire."

"Do we still have the same people working here as we did while I was serving as king—before I was captured and deposed?"

"Mostly, sire. Probably the biggest change is that Fitzroy is no longer here."

"What happened to him?"

"I'm not sure. He suddenly disappeared and was replaced by a woman named Tybatha. That's all I know."

Kylandar nodded, again waved to the others, and joined Max at the foot of the stairs. Together they ascended to King Kylandar's office on the third floor of the palace.

"It's good to be back home," Kylandar remarked as he looked around his quarters.

"Yes, Your Majesty. I agree."

The two men walked through Kylandar's suite of rooms before returning to his office. The king sat down in his chair behind his desk and motioned for Max to sit in a chair facing the desk.

"You said you would tell me what happened to Bynum when we got to the palace. Well, we're here—and I am most anxious to hear all the gory details of how you got rid of Bynum and the other demons."

"There's really not all that much to tell, Your Majesty. Since I had the coordinates to a spot in front of this desk, I had Vicky transport me right here. I kinda took Bynum by surprise and was able to send him back to Abaddon. Then I did the same thing to his wife, Tybatha. I searched the rest of the palace but could find no other demons. I'm just glad that Count DeVil wasn't around, since I'm not sure I would have been able to defeat him."

Kylandar sat still for several minutes, his head resting on his left hand as he silently studied Max. Finally he shook his head and said, "I'm sorry, Max—but that just won't cut it."

"What do you mean?"

"I mean you're leaving out too many details. I said I want *all* the gory details, but you've barely presented a quick summary."

"I've told you what I know. If you're wanting more details, let me try to answer your questions."

"All right, Max. Let's start with what I saw but still don't understand. When our army met the demonic forces of Abaddon, we all verbally agreed that we had no idea how we could defeat the ghostlike demons that could enter people's bodies and take possession of their minds, since they weren't affected by any of our weapons."

"I remember."

"Yet we didn't end up fighting them. Instead, an unusual storm suddenly appeared and conveniently destroyed our enemies with precisely aimed hailstones and lightning. I've never seen a storm that violent also be so precise and selective as to whom it killed. When I asked you about it, all you said was that you thought heavenly forces used the storm to destroy demons that had overstepped their bounds by leaving Abaddon."

"Yes, Your Majesty. That's what I think may have happened."

"Sorry, Max, but that's just not a satisfactory explanation—especially after you were able to single-handedly defeat both Bynum and Tybatha. I want more details."

"All right. I'll try to answer whatever questions you have."

"First, tell me what bounds you think the demons may have overstepped by leaving Abaddon and entering Ventryvia."

"Well, Your Majesty, Abaddon is a place that's been prepared for God's enemies, which includes demons confined there. I suspect they overstepped their bounds by escaping."

"God? Which god?"

"The only true God. The one who created everything."

"I've heard people talk about various gods, but I've never met any of them—so which one are you talking about? Does this god have a name?"

"He gave his name as being 'YHWH' in an ancient language. It roughly translates as being 'I AM' or 'I AM who I choose to be.'"

"Never heard of him before—but you think this particular god may have caused the storm that wiped out our enemies?"

"Yes, sire."

"Why?"

"He's the God I believe in and worship. The night before we moved out to engage the demons, I spent a lot of time in prayer to him—and I was rewarded with the most spectacular dream I've ever had. In the dream I was told to have faith in God, and then I watched the angelic armies of heaven fly into battle with the demons and destroy them the same way the storm later did as we watched. Was it just a crazy dream? Maybe. But I personally think God was telling me to trust in him. And I think he caused the storm and used it to destroy the demons."

Kylandar sat back in his chair and studied Max for several minutes while thinking through Max's answer. Finally he leaned forward and said, "All right. I'll accept that answer . . . at least for now. But tell me how you single-handedly got rid of both Bynum and Tybatha."

"Soulfire."

"What was that you said?"

"Soulfire. I can't explain it because I don't understand it, but the commander of God's angelic armies gave me this knife"—and Max pulled out the knife— "and told me to use it to direct soulfire at Bynum."

"How does it work?"

"I have no idea. All I know is that when Bynum was about to kill me, I pointed the knife at him and willed him to be destroyed or be gone. A bright light surrounded him and he disappeared. I then did the same thing to his wife."

Kylandar shook his head as if he were attempting to dislodge cobwebs. "I don't know, Max. I just don't know what to think. I'm glad you were victorious, of course. And I'm happy to be back in my palace among friends and to not have demonic forces disrupting everything. But I still don't feel as if I have a handle on what happened. I may ask you more questions later as I think of them."

"I understand, Your Majesty."

Max exited the king's office and went down the stairs to his own quarters on the second floor of the palace. After examining and reexamining his rooms and furnishings, he turned his attention to working with the power generators and solar panels he had installed on the roofs of the palace. He had started that work the preceding year but had been interrupted when King Kylandar had been abducted by Count DeVil's demons.

In a land largely controlled by magic, there was simply too much that could go wrong not to have essential systems backed up by other systems. Max therefore worked diligently with Vicky, his VIC3700 vocal interface computer, to safeguard and back up his wireless communication and computer systems.

Although Max worked diligently at his tasks, he wasn't working as meticulously or competently as normal—and that fact was not lost on the computer.

"What's wrong, sir?"

"What do you mean?"

"That's the fourth time you have incorrectly connected that cable, sir. It seems obvious your mind is not fully on what you are doing. Is something wrong?"

"Oh, I just keep thinking about Kylandar's questions and my responses."

"What do you mean?"

"I want to be open and fully honest with him—but there are some things I just can't tell him."

"Such as?"

"I can't tell him I'm actually an alien from another planet without jeopardizing both my mission and my friendship with him and the other friends I have here in Ventryvia. What would they do if they knew I had been sent here by Earth's Space Exploration Program to explore the planet and send back reports to Mission Control? I'm basically a spy rather than a citizen of their country."

"That hasn't kept you from aiding him or becoming his friend."

"No, it hasn't. At least not yet. So far I've been able to hide that fact. Kylandar and the others have simply regarded our machines and advanced technology as being a type of magic that differs from the magic they've grown up with and have utilized all their lives. They look upon me as being just another wizard even though I've told them I don't really know true magic."

"That's worked, hasn't it?"

"Yes, it's worked so far. I've even been able to answer his questions about God. But I can't tell him everything. For example, I can't tell him about the personal relationship I have with God."

"Why not?"

"Don't you see? My personal relationship was established when I accepted Jesus as my savior—but he was born, lived, and died on Earth—a planet far away from here. Any mention of that reveals that I'm an alien spy. I really like Kylandar, Rhylene and the others and want to be honest with them. But I can't do it without destroying everything. That's the quandary I'm facing, and I don't know what to do about it."

"Sorry, sir, but I'm not programmed to answer that for you."

If you enjoyed *Kings and Vagabonds,*
read on for a preview of

Joseph's Quest

A historical fiction novel
by Bill Kincaid

If you enjoyed Kings and Vagabonds,
read on for a preview of

Joseph's Quest

A historical fiction novel
by Bill Kincaid

Joseph lay at the bottom of a pit. His head and left shoulder hurt from where they had collided with rocks on his way down. Blood oozed from a gash in his left arm. His voice was hoarse from screaming for help. But mostly he was shocked, dazed and scared.

He had initially been upset, angry and incredulous that his own brothers would even think of attacking him. *How dare they do such a thing? Boy, will they ever catch it when Dad finds out! I can't wait to tell him. He'll fix them. Revenge will be sweet!*

But as he considered his fate and his limited options, fear replaced disbelief, though the desire for revenge and the shock of it all remained in full force. *Throwing me into this pit is a serious enough offense they might think they can't afford to let Dad find out. What if they just leave me here—or worse. They could kill me. No one would ever know. Dad didn't know they had left Shechem and come up here to Dothan.*

Joseph's brothers had stripped him of the ornamented tunic he had been wearing, leaving him almost naked when they threw him into the pit. "Stupid!" Joseph muttered to himself. *It was stupid of me to wear that tunic. I knew they were jealous of me for being Dad's favorite son—and wearing that multicolored coat just emphasized to them that I get preferential treatment.*

From where he lay at the bottom of the abandoned cistern, Joseph could hear his brothers talking as they ate. "What should we do with dreamer boy?" one of them asked. Joseph perked up to hear their words better.

"Reuben said for us not to shed his blood," someone else answered. The voice might have been Judah's, but Joseph wasn't sure.

"Yeah, but Reuben's not here now. What if the kid gets out of the pit and snitches on us again?" *Ah, that sounds like Dan.*

"He won't get out," another said. "Simeon tied up his hands real good."

"I agree. Simeon's knots hold."

"But we're talking about Joseph. He might dream up some way of getting out."

"Ha! Dreams!" a brother laughed. "That's what helped put him in that pit."

"Let's see how well his dreams turn out if he dies down there."

Joseph drew in a quick breath. *That was another stupid thing I did. Actually, several stupid things if you count the various times I boasted to my brothers about my dreams of their bowing down to me. Did I really think they would be positively impressed by being told such things? Dumb!*

Joseph turned so he could look up at the cistern walls. The roots and jagged rocks that extended from the sides might offer places where he could wedge hands or feet. But the walls sloped inward toward the narrow opening at the top of the cistern, and his hands were tied in such a way they were almost useless. Joseph looked around for something to use as a knife—but found nothing.

He did hear something, though: His brothers were talking excitedly. At first their words were too quiet for Joseph to understand. But as he strained to catch the words, he heard one brother exclaim, "Yes, I'm sure it's a caravan of camels coming from the direction of Gilead—probably Ishmaelites headed for Egypt."

"Listen, brothers. I've got a great idea."

"What is it, Judah?"

"What do we gain by killing our brother and covering up his blood? After all, he is our brother, our own flesh."

"Yeah—but what do you have in mind?"

"Come, let us sell him to the Ishmaelites. That way we make money, and we don't do away with him ourselves."

"Yeah. His blood won't be on our hands, and we also get paid."

The sounds of the caravan got louder, and then new voices and accents were added to the mix. When Joseph looked up, he saw a circle of strange faces looking down at him from the top of the cistern.

My brothers really and truly are trying to sell me as a slave to these foreigners. That's insane! That's detestable! That's ... That's ... That's ... probably better than the other option I heard them discussing. It's obvious they won't let me go free for fear of what I'll tell Dad. Being a slave will at least keep me alive with a chance for escaping at some point. Then I can plot my revenge for what they've done to me.

"God, help me and please stay with me," Joseph prayed as he saw Judah being lowered into the pit on a rope. Judah wrapped both the end of the rope and his own arms around Joseph, signaled to their brothers, and both men were lifted out of the pit.

"Well, here he is," Levi said to the Ishmaelites. "As you can see, he's a strong and healthy lad of seventeen years. He can work all day."

The Ishmaelites examined Joseph from head to toe, checked his teeth, and felt of his muscles. Then they huddled and discussed him in a language Joseph couldn't understand. Finally one of them turned to the brothers and said, "We'll give you ten pieces of silver for him."

"Ten?" gasped Judah. "He's worth at least fifty. You're not going to find a better or more intelligent slave anywhere for that price."

"Don't try that line on us," said one of the traders. "You boys are desperate to get rid of him. We'll take him off your hands and pay you fifteen pieces of silver. You're in no position to bargain."

Judah looked at his brothers and mouthed a number. When they nodded, he turned and said, "Thirty."

"Twenty—and that's our last offer. Take it or we leave him with you."

Joseph's brothers looked at each other, nodded, and took the offer. The Ishmaelites counted out twenty shekels of silver, put a rope around Joseph's wrists, attached the other end of the rope to a wagon, and led him away.

Made in the USA
Middletown, DE
29 July 2024